MARKED

TRIBES, #1

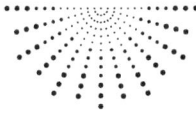

MILANA JACKS

CHAPTER ONE

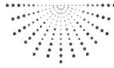

HART

Another night falls over our territory. Another night of peace after the brutal tribal wars that have ravaged our lands, killed thousands of males, destroyed the females, and completely eliminated any hope for the young.

I flick the dirt from under my claw, hoping the Alpha of the neighboring Ra tribe feels how I feel, devastated, hopeless, and ready to wage more wars, because, if the ritual doesn't bear fruit, I'm gonna break the truce and march into his territory, destroy every one of them.

My males file into the Hall of the Fallen and gather around the fire. Smoke rises and envelops the room. I wanna plug my nose so I don't inhale, but I have to inhale for the spirit of Bera, goddess of fertility, to enter my body. Or some nonsense like that the Sha-male spouts, which my people eat up like raw flesh in our mouths.

I've lost faith in our goddess of fertility. Send me Amti, goddess of madness and lust, and let her consume my body so I can devour and kill until someone bests me and puts me out of my misery.

Fuck, I'm dramatic.

1

Chuckling, I glance at the Sha.

He's still drawing on the same wall he's been drawing on every span for a cycle straight. He's got faith and perseverance, I'll give him that. But I'm sick of inhaling the prayer smoke that makes my brain fuzzy, and I know for a fact my males are coming for the smoke too. This has to stop.

"Sha," I say as I rise from the throne. "Tonight is the last night."

A wrinkled hand holding the brush pauses, but the male doesn't turn. He continues painting.

"Sha-male, I know you heard me."

"Yes, Alpha. I'm not deaf."

My males laugh.

I cut them a look because I'm in a foul mood, and no amount of smoke from the fire is gonna calm me down. I'm done with the rituals. I approach the Sha and lean a shoulder on the wall.

He gives me a side-eye. "Go sit by the fire. Your anger and impatience scares Bera."

"Maybe she'll appear just to tame me." I grab my crotch.

Sha drops the brush and wipes his hands on his black apron. "That's it. You've ruined the night." He pokes me in the chest. "But know this, mighty Hart, when the females enter our lands, you will be the last to breed one."

"The females can't enter our lands. There aren't any left to walk the lands."

"There must be." Tears appear in the old man's eyes, and now I feel bad for slapping him with reality, telling him his hopes and our faith in goddesses won't bring back any of the females slain in the wars. It won't breed new ones either, and females don't just fall from the sky.

Gently, I place a hand on his fragile shoulder. "Go take a whiff of Bera's body and jerk off for the night." The Sha are chaste. I'm a hookhead through and through.

He walks away.

I turn toward my males. Their eyelids drape their eyes. Some males even hang their heads.

Mas, our portal genius, looks up, licks his dry lips. "I've prepared the terrain for the games."

I snort. Even with all the technological advances, even with the world he's seen, he still believes Bera will bless us with a female, and the games must be prepared for the female's arrival.

In the tribe, males compete for the right to breed a female. May the strongest male win and give the next generation's best chance of survival. Even if I don't believe, even if I've lost faith, I have to allow the preparations, if only so I don't appear as if I'm following in my father's footsteps.

Instead of competing in the games, deeming them useless, he snatched my mother and marked her so no other male could have her. In hiding, she delivered him two sons before the Ra tribal Alpha, the Rai at the time, delivered her my father's head. Since the Rai couldn't breed her, he killed her, but not before she hid me and my brother. We grew up and sought vengeance that led to more vengeance and then some more, and before we knew it, a decade of violence had passed.

I approach the fire, part my verto, and piss on it. The fire dies out, and all hope dies with it. "I'm going to hunt. Maybe kill something. Who wants to come?" Males rise and follow me outside. They'd follow me anywhere, so I better lead them to the land of prosperity, not ruin.

CHAPTER TWO

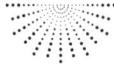

STEPHANIE

M y vacation to Joylius sure started out exciting.

First, the ship caught fire. Then the captain initiated the emergency passenger rescue protocol, meaning each seat on the ship got enclosed in a steel globe that could prevent us from burning up in the atmosphere and withstand a hard landing. What I didn't expect was to be ejected into space right before the ship exploded.

"Approaching land," the pod's autopilot says.

Oh, thank God. I lean back in the chair and strap in for the landing. Thankfully, these rescue pods self-navigate, and I don't have to do anything but sit back and recall my existence while the pod self-navigates to the nearest land or a space station, whatever it can find. I presume it's Joylius, a human colony, since that's where the ship was headed in the first place, though I fear I might be wrong now that I've breached the clouds and the landscape isn't what a vacation spot on Joylius should look like.

I've only ever gone to the resorts, and this could be the metropolis on Joylius, for all I know. It's a green city with several expansive structures that have oval rooftops like the Taj Mahal, and strange, tall, uneven, narrow black towers that rise from the ground like trees might on Earth.

As the pod approaches one of the towers, I see people roaming the unpaved streets. While Joylius natives aren't humanoid, humans have colonized the planet, so I must be in the right place. The pod stops and hovers in front of one tower. I presume it's requesting to dock, and I wait. And wait a bit more, tapping my fingernail on my front tooth. If I didn't have a new French manicure, I'd likely bite the nail. "Hey computer, what's going on."

The lights in the pod shut off.

I look around. "Hello?"

The pod drops.

I scream at the top of my lungs, shut my eyes, and say a Hail Mary before I leave this mortal plane and hopefully end up somewhere in Heaven even though I lied to my boss, telling him my mother was sick so he'd approve my vacation request. My mother remarried and is living a good life on Mars. She wouldn't see me even if she were sick anyway.

The pod halts, the pressure in my ears pops, and my belly ends up in my throat from the sudden change. I snap open my eyes. The pod didn't crash. Thank God. This is good. Very good. My restraints come off, the small exit door pops open, and I'm finally free to leave the confined space. I've never been claustrophobic, but spending half a day confined inside a tiny sphere took a toll on my psyche. I want to spend the rest of my vacation in an open space, thank you very much. Maybe I'll sleep on the beach and not even check into my room.

My body protests the move from the chair. I groan as my ass unglues itself from the leather and stretch my leg to step outside. Looking around, I see a…a path in front of me that takes me to massive iron double doors attached to a building that's not round. This one has sharp edges, like thorns sticking out of a wide towerlike structure.

The pod lifts and leaves.

"Hey!" I shout after it. "Come back! I didn't get my purse." It's gone in a second. I can barely see it attaching to one of the towers on my right. Sighing, I head toward the tower that holds the pod, but stop moving once I see what's in the street in front of me.

Massive, bulky alien males who took their fashion sense from the Vikings have formed a living wall. Fur, axes, daggers, leather kilts, tattoos on their faces and bodies, some even on their heads. Not Joylius natives for sure, and while they look human, they're not. Their jaws are too rigid, and their eyes are covered with a white membrane as if they're all blind. I have no idea if they are, though I doubt it as I see their heads move up and down as they take in my appearance.

I don't think this is my vacation planet.

Several of them step forward. I step back and notice movement under the skin on their chest and arms, as if something is moving inside them. One male speaks, but his language doesn't translate.

"I am a human," I say. "From Earth. Is this Joylius?" I doubt it. National Security wouldn't allow vacations on Joylius if they knew about these males. They look like warrior-class aliens. We either war against them or with them against the common enemy, namely any alien classified as predator.

The male who stepped forward drops to all fours and leans forward, making loud sniffing noises, moving his nose left and right in a way humans can't. Another male follows, and another, and the three of them look like wolves ready to snatch a rabbit. Rabbits run, and my heart starts beating faster, legs moving back while the males follow, slowly as if not to scare me. One male's muscles start bulging, stretching his skin. His jaw drops, showing me his canines. Fuck this.

I spin and run as fast as my legs will carry me up the path that looks like a bridge now and toward those double doors that open for me. Seeking shelter, I pump my legs across the bridge and enter a giant hall surrounded by tall windows.

Behind me, the doors start closing, and I turn and see the males on the bridge. I have nowhere to go. On all fours, the males creep toward me, their muscles and bones stretching their skin as if something wants to break free from inside them. Is that even possible? I don't know. I've never seen humanoids like this before.

The doors close with a whoosh, and I back off a little and take in the doors. There are patterns carved into them, with a few repeating ones, sort of like tribal markings, for lack of a better comparison. The scent, similar to frankincense, reminds me of church. I walk around the place while my knees shake, threatening to collapse. I need an exit or a weapon. Preferably an exit. Neither appears.

It's an empty hall with intricate mosaics on the floors, exotic, even charming, the kind of luxury my mother would appreciate. Even on the walls, there's art, but none depicting people. Just lots of colors and patterns, most of them quite feminine: flowers; elegant cursive lines. Seductive in a strange way.

I stub my toe on something and trip. Hands out, I prevent a face plant, then rise back up, wiping my palms on my jeans.

Steps.

Duh.

I climb them, fascinated by the floor and the patterns so much that I don't see him until I lift my head.

A male sits on a throne that wasn't here just minutes ago when I entered and surveyed the room. His shoulders are as wide as the throne and covered in a fur vest that closes with leather laces crossing in the front. Over his long black kilt, he wears a golden belt with the same repeating patterns I saw on the door. Abundant long black hair is secured away from his face, clearly showing tribal-like tattoos over his jawbone and up his face, stopping at his cheeks. Pupilless white eyes stare back at me.

I think he's a...a king or a president or something like that, so I do what most humans do when presented with alien royalty: I bow my head. "Hi, my name is Stephanie, and I'm a human from Earth."

Banging against the doors startles me, and I look up. The males outside are shouting in their native tongue, which seems to be spoken from the chest and back of the throat, so we're gonna have a hard time communicating with no translators.

He appears in front of me. He's so fast, his movements are a blur.

Shit. I step back.

He doesn't follow. He leans forward and sniffs, does a weird lifting and moving of his nose. My scent seems to confuse him, because he frowns, then drops to all fours, eyes still locked with mine. He sniffs closer to my belly, then down and between my legs.

I'm horrified, probably tomato faced. Luckily, the horrid identification his species uses when met with another species ends quickly, and he stands, returning to his seat.

Oh good.

The doors start opening, and I turn to see an army of males lining the bridge, waiting for the doors to open all the way so they can barge in here after me. Not good.

I run behind the throne, hit the wall, then run back, and

because I'm desperate, I crouch behind the throne, repeating the Hail Mary, eyes closed, awaiting an unpleasant fate.

I don't know what they're gonna do with me, but aliens classified as warriors tend to be rather hostile. Maybe I'm a prisoner now. Maybe they hope to trade me for some of our tech. Maybe they'll just kill me.

CHAPTER THREE

HART

My males rush into the Hall of the Fallen, chasing after our prey, Sor in the lead. He's just leapt over the steps when I stand and sock him in the jaw. His head snaps back, spinning his body, but he flips and manages to land on his feet. Bones rearrange, align, and snap back together, taking him out of the hunter and back into a male.

He rubs his jaw and glares at me. "The hunt is fair game. You didn't hunt."

"The prey walked into my lair."

"That's not how it works. We hunted, and I'm first. You have to honor the winner."

"The prey outran you."

My males laugh, and Sor smirks. "You're joking, I see. Get out of my way."

I shake my head. "That's not how it works either. You want the prey, you come and take her from me." I expect Sor to back off, not because he's scared he'll lose the fight, but because we can't afford to fight each other over food. The unidentified species is clearly food, and we have plenty of that.

He throws up his hands. "Fine, but I want the leg and a buttock. Big buttocks, it looked like. Yummy." He rubs his belly.

"I agree. Now, let me eat."

My males file out of the hall, and I round the throne to find the prey looking up at me with big colored eyes. Crouching in front of her—and it's a female judging by the scent between her legs—I examine the round black dot in her eye surrounded by a lovely shade of brown, a warm hue we'd use to color our bedrooms or places of worship. I lean in some more, and the black dot in her eye widens. I lean back. What was that? I lean in, and it widens. Lean back again. Shrinks. I do this several times because it's fun, and I'm toying a bit with my food.

For us, the predators, the process of identifying food is simple. We smell the prey, and I sniff, my nose telling me she's edible. Sniffing again, I detect a male in the hall. I stand and inhale again, sorting through the scents of my males to identify him. It's Sor again. He won't try to steal the food from me because he knows he'll die, so why is he still lingering? I don't like it, so I growl. He growls back. I think he's hungry and irrational, and I'd hate to kill him for trying to steal my food. Instead of snarling and chasing him out, I press the dial on my throne.

The throne drops into my chambers, right under the Hall of the Fallen. The prey bends forward and hacks, putting a hand over her mouth. Is she sick? Maybe. The turbulence in the pod must've been unpleasant, and the hunt scared her. It'll be over fast. I'll make it quick and painless. It is a female after all, and I'm softer on female prey than male prey.

"Who are your people?" I ask, hoping she'll understand me. Most times, aliens caught and brought here for consumption have translators already, but I don't think this one does. She wipes her mouth, her strange brown eyes looking around my chambers. She speaks in a way that requires lots of tongue movement, so her language with no translator would be difficult for me to mimic.

Why would I want to mimic this language? Frowning, I walk to the command center and sense her movement. I turn to see her running. Every instinct in my body screams *chase*, but if I do, I'll consume her too quickly and forget I promised Sor a leg. And a buttock. There's no way he's getting a buttock, though. Those are nice big juicy buttocks.

Makes me wanna look at her some more. It's a female alien, and it's…attractive, with a pleasing sweet scent between her legs. I want to smell her some more. Maybe eat later. I'm not that hungry anyway. Besides, there's nowhere to go down here in the same way there's nowhere to go up in the hall or any place where we corner our prey.

Our structures are designed to attract prey and make it easy for us to corner them. Some of us toy with prey, give them hope, let them think they can escape, but most of us don't. It's a bit sadistic when you're eating something that still smells like hope. Though this prey doesn't smell hopeful as she runs around tapping the walls that reveal no exits.

She reaches the window, taps around, then shouts something and bangs on the glass. Quietly, I approach, and she turns around and plasters her body against the window, tongue and lips moving rapidly. She's talking a lot, and based on my experience with cornered prey, I'm guessing she's most likely begging. She freezes as I reach beside her to unlatch the window and open it so she can see there's no way out of here unless she's an experienced climber or has wings.

A pleasant scent catches my interest, so I linger, sniffing around her hair before pulling back, but not stepping away from her.

She doesn't turn to look out the window.

We stand there facing each other while her body trembles.

I take her hand and observe clawless fingers. I lift her upper lip to see blunt teeth. Herbivore.

The wind blows through the window and ruffles her hair. I release it from the band and let it fall down to her shoulders. Since the prey is rather small, I bend to sniff the top of her head. It also smells sweet, but with a different scent than the place between her legs. Interesting. Instead of dry showering like most species who can travel through space, this species uses oils to clean themselves with, like us. I'm not familiar with the particular scent of her hair, but it's not offensive to my sensitive nose either. In fact, it's undeniably pleasant.

The female grabs my ax and yanks it out of my belt. I step back, expecting her to swing, but the ax proves too heavy for her and she drops it, cutting the side of her thigh in the process. She yelps and covers her wound. Blood seeps between her fingers and calls to me. I drop to all fours, my hunter at the ready, muscles already relaxing to allow for bones to rearrange. My vision sharpens, and I home in on the red blood.

I lick her fingers, lapping the sweet nectar, then move her hands out of the way so I can taste straight from the source. Her fear overwhelms my senses as I rip the soft blue fabric she's wearing and lap at the cut, purring as I taste the sweetest blood I've ever tasted in my life. I imagine what her meat tastes like and nip her wound gently, toying with but not breaking the skin. I lap and lap, and two things happen that have never happened when I'm trying to prime my prey for consumption.

One, I grow hard.

Two, I purr in a way I don't understand. The tone is

wrong. I'm not a happy hunter readying to eat; I'm something else I can't quite put my finger on.

I stare at the wound. Instead of ripping out her flesh, I healed her cut. It's completely closed, and I'm a little annoyed that I unconsciously released a wound-sealing saliva. It was an instinctual behavior and one that came from my hunting instincts. Why would I do that?

Standing, I narrow my eyes at the female, who lifts her thigh to examine it. She runs a blunt finger over her cut and looks up, speaking something I can't understand again. I'm starting to get annoyed that I don't understand her while she's pointing at the ax. What was she gonna do with the ax? Cut me or put herself out of her misery?

I already tasted her, and instead of consuming her, I healed her. It could mean only one thing, and I'm reluctant to even hope it is what it could be. Let's find out what she'd intended to do.

I pick up the ax and put it back into her hand. This time, I hold it with her and firmly direct it to the side of my neck, lifting my chin to expose my throat. Her hand still shakes, the ax proving too heavy once more, so I hold her elbow to help support the weapon.

She's calculating. I can tell. Her brown eyes dart from my face to my throat, and I can see the moment she decides to move in for the kill.

The female grabs the ax with both hands and cuts.

The scent of my blood bursts into the room, and I purr, strangely aroused by her violence. The Sha might've succeeded in his ritual, and Bera might've actually given us a female to breed. I tug the ax from her, holster it, and lift her upper lip to take a peek at her teeth again. Definitely an herbivore. A violent herbivore. What in Herea's name kind of creature is this? Regardless, we can't breed prey, and we definitely can't produce young with herbivores, so she's of no use to me besides food in my belly. And yet, my instincts tell me to keep her around a little longer.

I purse my lips, thinking on what to do, not wanting to make decisions before I'm certain she's just an herbivore. She could be one of those strange omnivorous creatures who eat both flesh, bone, and herbs, in which case, she might be the female Bera sent us. Only one way to find out. Take the alien hunting.

CHAPTER FOUR

STEPHANIE

The alien male purrs. Trouble is, he purrs the way a giant tiger might purr, not like a domestic cat might if I pet it. I won't pet him, and the cut on his neck keeps bleeding. He healed me with his tongue, which he can't do for himself, and I'd rather make friends than enemies, especially since I can't kill him with his ax. It's heavy, made for his strength, and I couldn't even swing it. But that didn't stop me from cutting him. I have to stand my ground.

His purr intensifies, and he keeps stepping closer, and I can't back off because the window is open and I'll fall out if I move. He's cornering me, I realize. I have no way to escape, and as his body touches mine, I feel his hardness.

Right past him, a large elaborate bed dominates the massive space, surrounded by tiny lights like stars, warm and inviting, twinkling in some places. The space seems private, and I grow more apprehensive of what this kind of place implies. Originally, I thought he would rip my thigh out with his teeth, so the fact he didn't, both gives me hope and worries me.

As a show of good will, I slip out of my shirt, leaving me

in the tank top. I twist the shirt and extend my hands, trying to reach his neck. He's tall, and I can't reach the wound even when I rise on my toes. He bends slightly, and I'm happy we're communicating so easily with no translator. I tie the cloth around his neck to stop the bleeding. "There," I say. "Can I get back to my pod now?"

He shows me his canines, and I swallow at the sight of a set of teeth made for ripping flesh and crushing bone. But his eyes lift at the corners, so I have a feeling he's smiling. I smile back, and he bends again to look at my teeth. It's then that I notice something behind the whiteness of his eyes. Maybe the pupil is behind there and also a colored iris. I can't tell, but I see it moving. It's as creepy as the way his body moves under the skin.

Aliens come in all shapes and forms, and while I haven't seen one like this one, it doesn't mean they don't exist. It means I haven't seen as much of the universe as I'd like.

Space travel doesn't come cheap, and the only reason I could afford the vacation on Joylius was because the tsunami hit it recently and wiped out all but two resorts. This prompted them to drop prices on space fare and hotels, so it came within my budget.

The male takes my hand into his warm one. He's hot, actually, his natural temperature much higher than mine. He leads me back to the throne. The disk the throne is on spins once and catapults up, lifting my belly in the process. I hold in the bile this time. I'm not as nauseated as I was after I landed and ran from a herd of males chasing me.

The disk stops in the throne room. Without pausing to adjust to the sudden launch and stop, he leads me forward, and when the doors swing open, I sigh, relieved the bridge is empty.

We walk. Below us, water gushes, hitting the stone structure. On the street, clusters of massive warriors like him chat in their strange language, and above, ships fly to and from the towers. I focus on one tower and see a white dot up there that looks like my pod. I point to it. "That's the one."

The alien nods and moves toward the tower, passing all those males that chased me. They get out of his way, but my belly feels queasy at the glances they're throwing my way and how they're licking their lips. It makes me uncomfortable, especially as I don't see any women anywhere. In fact, I don't see kids either, or animals, or anything besides scarred, muscular males with long beaded braids hanging over their bare chests, white eyes turning my way. They wear what I presume is their uniform of scuffed leather kilts hung with powerful weapons.

Warrior species tend to be military species, so I'm not surprised they're carrying many weapons, but still, where are the civilians in this town? Unless, this is some sort of military stronghold I landed in, which would be unfortunate mostly because lots of species designate humans as enemies. We have a terrible habit of capturing and experimenting on aliens before we reach out and make friendly contact.

The excuse is that, prior to letting aliens know about humanity, we have to be sure they're not predators. Aliens classified as predators are either kept from discovering our species, barred from entering our space, or, if they find out about us and want to approach, we call our allies and kill them off.

A male steps in front of us, and although his gaze is downcast, he speaks loudly and sounds angry. The one with me replies in kind. A snarl rips out of him, and I startle, trying to jerk my hand away. He glares, eyes no longer covered in white. They're bright orange with vertical slits for pupils. I freeze in place.

My bladder threatens to release both from fear and because I have to go. I press my thighs together, then stare at the ground, mainly because I feel I did something wrong when I tried to pull away. I won't be doing that anymore. I squeeze his warm hand.

The other male moves out of the way, and we continue walking. Under his breath, the male mumbles, and I bet he's cursing. Or maybe not. Shit. I know nothing of anything in this place, and that's reaffirmed when the alien passes the tower I believe we're gonna enter. I look up at him, ready to open my mouth and seek answers, but there's no point because he doesn't understand me. I wish he'd get me a translator.

"I need a translator," I say.

He gives me a side-eye, and I run two fingers over my throat, then touch my lips. "A translator." Most species understand this signal. Two fingers on the throat, then lips, and I think he does too, because he nods and picks up the pace.

Next to him, I'm practically running as we weave through the streets at a frantic pace. I try to make sense of what I'm seeing. The farther we get from the place I landed, the more I feel like something terrible happened here and that's why there aren't any civilians.

We pass homes with damaged rooftops, broken doors, and smeared paint over the art normally found on most of the walls I've seen in this place. Right after seeing a street bustling with warriors and air traffic, the silence here makes me wary. On the ground, right next to a pile of weapons, I spot a massive animal skull with teeth as big as my finger. Then another, covered in mold. A crisp breeze brushes my hair, and I inhale stale air and the stench of standing water. It appears to be an abandoned village, perhaps now a cemetery, as if the ancient Vikings raided the town and nobody repaired it since. I wonder if something similar actually happened here.

The male starts jogging.

Unable to keep up with him, I tug on his hand.

He flings me into the air, and I land on top of some sort of broad-backed creature that's in the middle of the street. It starts running with me clamping my legs around its flanks. Screaming at the top of my lungs, I hang on tight to whatever I can grab on the creature. My fingers clench around a cloth tied at the creature's neck. It's my twisted shirt. Oh my God! This male is a dual-form species, meaning he's both humanoid and animal, and I better hold on for a ride or die as we gallop at breakneck speed.

He leaps, and I duck my head, shutting my eyes and not wanting to see what he's leaping over. I'm scared of heights and speeds and, well, many things he's clearly not afraid of.

Landing roughly, he stops. My cheek bounces off the muscle on his back, and I lose my grip on the cloth, then bounce off him and fall flat on my ass.

Grunting, I move to stand, but think better of it. I stay down because the male chooses to remain in his animal form, and he's practically pinning me down with his dominant stare. Narrow vertical pupils. Bright orange eyes. He's the size of a horse, with a massive head and exposed teeth, meaning there're no lips over the teeth. They're out here for all to see, each canine the size of my middle finger. His coat is black, with short thick hair and large ears that stick out and make him seem even bigger. He's built strong and agile, with back legs in a folded position sort of like a frog, which explains the massive leap he executed.

Leaning in, he sniffs between my legs again.

"Please stop doing that, because it's freaking me out. Also, I have to pee." Standing on shaky legs, I try not to appear afraid. I struggle to calm my racing heart because I know *class: Predator* scents fear, and they generally wanna devour the ones who fear them. My bladder makes it easy to forget the fear. I gotta go. Luckily, we landed in a forest.

I force my legs to move and walk to the nearest bush in front of a wide tree trunk. The grass that grows around the base of the tree is oval shaped and seems softer than California grass, and the forest smells wonderful from all the different flowers that grow on the trees. Red, yellow, even neon blue. It's like a magical place, and I'm sad I have to desecrate it with my urine, but a girl's gotta do what a girl's gotta do.

I squat and am going about my business when the alien animal's head pokes around the bush. Bright orange eyes widen, and his pupils shrink into tiny slits.

"Shoo." I motion with my hand, but to him, that must have looked like I invited him over, because he circles the bush and stands there, staring at me. I can't stop what I need to do, so I'm doing it, and I'm mortified when his head lowers, and he watches the flow. Since I haven't gone in hours, it takes me eighty-four years to finish up. I squeeze every last drop out of me and promptly dress, then step away from the spot.

The second I do, he draws near and sniffs the place. I'm trying to be less human about this and draw out my animal side too, if only to make myself feel better about this turn of events, and not think about how, if I stay here longer than a few hours, I'll need to be escorted to the bathroom again and go through this embarrassing process, also again.

The male glances at me, then at the pee, lifts a leg, and pisses on the same spot.

He swings his long whiplike tail, wrapping it around my leg like a cat might, and swaggers off, throwing his head back in a way that clearly says *follow me*.

Grumbling, I follow him through the forest, mainly

because I don't have a choice. As we walk, I try to forget about our private fluid exchange and admire the environment on this planet. There are markings carved into the tree trunks. Not as elaborate or purposeful as the ones I'd seen elsewhere, but natural forms that make them even more beautiful. As we walk, I try to preserve my life by drawing out his humanoid side. You know, the one that talks. I ask him many questions he can't answer without a translator, or maybe even with it because he remains in this animal form, but either way, he maintains a frightening silence. I wonder if he's taking me to his lair or a cave, or to a secret spot where he can finish me off.

CHAPTER FIVE

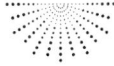

HART

Carnivores hunt. Omnivores eat plants or hunt for prey. This alien marked my territory, which I immediately corrected by pissing over her marking so that we establish order right away and she isn't confused about who here is predator and who is not.

I still can't believe she pissed on my territory. If she were anyone from my tribe, I'd have considered it a declaration of dominance and a definite challenge. If she were a Ra, it would have been a declaration of war.

Instead of doing what a normal hungry creature does in a forest rich with plant and animal life, the alien I'd brought here to eat talks and strolls as if we're walking through town. She must be confused. She's supposed to seek food, but she keeps touching the trees, picking flowers off them, and talking. Her tongue muscle gets plenty of exercise, and appears more agile than mine.

I stick out my tongue, looking at it hanging over the side of my teeth. It swings as I walk, practically an unused muscle for me. Unlike a few tribes in our land, we bite, crush, and swallow prey. Not much need for mixing food with the tongue. Her tongue maneuvering makes me think she's an herbivore more than anything else. The thought of her being an herbivore frustrates me, and I growl.

Night is falling, and since she's not hunting, and I can't hunt effectively with her, I better get back into town. The woods aren't safe in daylight, and at night, they're deadly. My hunters aren't the only ones who might wanna eat this alien.

I step in front of her and cut off her path, then swing my tail and hit my back with the tip, telling her to hop on. She stands there, hands full of flowers, and talks at me again. Huffing out a breath, I stroll beside her at her pace. Before taking her hunting, I should've gotten a translator. At the time, hunting took priority, because if she's an herbivore, we're incompatible, and I have to know what's what with this female.

We arrive at a portal that leads back into town from this position deeper inside the forest. Around this time, the portal security shift changes, and I nod at the pair of males on duty as we enter the portal. She stops as we hit the street again and talks, loudly now. From their positions around the streets, the males gawk at her. She's none the wiser. She's looking around while arranging a bouquet she collected. I snarl, a little annoyed they're all staring at her.

A group of males heads our way, and none of them even acknowledge me as they pass. A whistle sounds, and I spin, snapping my teeth at them. They scatter like cowards, laughing as they take positions around the towers. Bitch-holes. All of them.

I continue walking, feeling the alien staring at my ears.

I side-eye her and change back so I can speak. "They haven't seen a female in a while," I explain. "I have to stay vigilant." And maybe I'm a bit agitated, a tiny bit possessive, and definitely protective too, because I don't want anyone stealing my...food. That's all she is. My food. Smells good too. A cute walking piece of meat with colored eyes. But food nonetheless until further confirmation.

I can't mate with food. We are incompatible, even if I felt like pissing on her as I would on any hunter female I chose for breeding. In hunting form, it's easier to become confused, both the instinct to breed and the instinct to eat coming from the same place in the brain. I think better on two feet than on four.

I would not piss on her in this rational male state. I wouldn't.

My brother, Nar, rushes out of the tower and walks with me. I should've pissed on her. Instinctively, I throw my arm over the female and bring her closer. She protests and tries to move away, but I snarl at her too. Everyone is making me edgy this evening. Someone's gonna fill my belly, and I hope it's not her or my brother, because I will regret both those choices.

I can feel his gaze on the side of my face, practically piercing my cheek.

"You're escorting me to my chambers?" I ask.

"Mas is scrubbing the pod's data."

"And?"

"They eat flowers?" He makes a noise at the back of his throat. We're both grossed out that an alien species eats flowers, but it is what it is.

"Good question. I don't know. Tell me about the pod's data."

A corner of his lip lifts as if he's smiling, but I ignore it and nudge him with an elbow. "Don't make me ask again."

"The pod detached from the ship that carried it and proceeded according to preset coordinates."

"Where did they lead?"

"Our territory."

"What's Mas's working theory?"

"The Ra boarded her ship, and instead of consuming the prey, they placed them inside pods and sent them to the homeland. Her pod malfunctioned and ended up here."

"Why?"

"Why what?"

"Why send this one to the homeland?"

"For later consumption? I don't know. Clearly, she's an herbivore, so what else is there to do with her?"

I stop and give him my most bored look.

He frowns. "Did I miss something?"

I knock on his head. "Think outside the skull."

He nods, scrubbing his jaw. "Since we control the majority of the portals, the Ra are experiencing food short-ages, so some of them left the homeland on warbirds in search for food. They capture, board, and eat, and what they don't eat, they send home."

"I don't think she's food."

"What else would they send her home for?"

"Breeding."

He blinks, clearly having never considered it. We haven't seen a female in, well, most of our adult lifetime, so it makes sense that we don't consider it. It's a novelty for most of us, and the ritual is a bunch of crap only Sha believes in.

Nar slaps a hand on my shoulder, and I halt. He steps closer, and our chests touch. I growl because his dominance invades my senses. My muscles start relaxing, bones twitch-ing, eager to fight him. My brother would be a worthy oppo-nent, one who would fight to the death, which is why we never fight. There are just over one thousand Ka hunters left, and if we fight each other, we might as well sign off on our extinction.

"Breeding?" he whisper hisses and looks around as if we're exchanging territorial portal secrets. He knocks on my head and leans in to speak into my ear. "Are you crazy inside?"

I slap his hand away. "Look around. We're a dying breed, as are the Ra."

"They have females."

"Most aren't fertile anymore."

"Then you know what to do. If they're collecting breeders across the galaxy, then we might have a breeder in our midst, which is going to stir up the others for the games. You are the Kai, so you eat first, but when it comes to breeding, all males are born equal until one wins."

The winner takes the breeder. The losers have to wait for another game. There can be up to four hundred males competing in the games, so beating three hundred and ninety-nine of my males is akin to weakening my defenses. The moment the Ra hear about the games, they'll send their males, and since there's a truce, we have to allow them entry. "I'm aware."

"What will you do?"

"Nothing yet. She didn't hunt."

"And yet…" My brother touches his nose. "I smell your disappointment. You're not thinking about… Oh no, brother, don't do it. You fucking her and then consuming her is wrong. Sexy but wrong." Nar glances at my alien, who's unusually quiet, big brown eyes darting from me to him and finally resting on him, which makes me growl.

Nar steps back. "We're getting ahead of ourselves. She's clearly an herbivore, and you'll have a nice meal, and we'll forget all about this breeding conversation."

"She peed on my territory."

His eyes widen.

I nod. "Marked it right in front of me too. What kind of an herbivore marks a predator's territory?"

"A stupid herbivore."

"Didn't even dig a hole to hide the scent."

"Seriously?" He's as shocked as I was when I saw what she was doing.

I nod. "Just squatted and went."

"I'd have killed her for that. You can't have an herbivore marking our hunting grounds. That's...that's...unnatural."

"I have to investigate this alien. For the good of my people. You understand?"

Nah snorts. "What do you think the flowers are for?"

"I don't know."

"If she starts eating them, then you'll know, but before you know, don't speak of breeding." He taps my shoulder and finally prepares to leave. "Kai." He drops his gaze, respectfully.

"One more thing," I say. "Get me a translator."

Nar slaps his cheek. Once, twice, three times.

"What are you doing?"

"I'm trying to awaken from a bad dream where you want to talk to your food."

I chuckle. My brother is funny.

"Before Mas hands me the translator, he'll want to know why you want to speak with food. What do I tell him?"

"We're interrogating her for intel on Ra's warbird."

"Mas is scrubbing the pod, and it will tell him everything we need to know. Brother, please, let's just have dinner and be done with her. I have a bad feeling about this."

"I don't need a reason to ask for a translator. And if Mas doesn't give you one, tell him I will come and take his eye along with the translator. Have a pleasant evening."

CHAPTER SIX

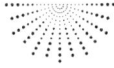

STEPHANIE

The entire time we walked, I kept searching for water or a vase where I could put these beautiful flowers, but as we make our way under the throne room, all hopes of finding anything go down the drain.

This time around, the throne shoots back up and closes the ceiling, darkening this space. I can barely see the male as he stands in the middle of the room. He waves his arms in front of him, agile fingers working on something I can't see. The lights come on. They're tiny yellow stars on the ceiling and walls.

A chill runs down my spine, and I shiver, rubbing my shoulder, still holding the flowers with the other hand. Nightstands pop up on both sides of the bed, a fireplace too, more art appears on the walls, and the lights dim.

The male ceases his frantic hand movements and watches me, scrubbing his jaw. He starts pacing, every once in a while throwing glances my way.

I signal, again requesting a translator, but he shakes his head, telling me either no, he won't provide me one, or that he doesn't understand. Frustrated, I throw up a hand and place the flowers on the nightstand, knowing with no water, they'll die by morning.

Outside the window, a strange moon rises, much bigger than our moon in the Solar System. It dawns on me that it's night, which means time to go to bed, but there's only one bed and literally no other place to crash but the cold floor. With no sheets anywhere in sight, I worry I might freeze.

The red beacons on the towers dim down too, and I barely see my pod under one light. Just sitting there, lonely and secluded from the rest of the ships docked around the tower. Kind of like me.

I don't hear him approach, but the heat of his body tells me he's behind me. I step into him and rub my back on his chest. "I'm thinking you don't sleep under covers because you don't need them. You don't wear many clothes either because you don't need them and also because you have a second form and the clothes might rip. I need covers, and I don't have a second form. I also need food and water. At least I have shelter. So that's good." For how long, though?

I spin around and look up into his white eyes. I can't see the orange or the pupil behind it now. "Why are you keeping me here?"

He speaks, his voice a deep baritone.

I sigh and move around him, then stand in front of the bed. Bending, I touch the floor. Nope. I'll freeze. I open the pair of nightstands made of that gorgeous wood, dark brown in color and warmer than the floor. Inside, there's nothing but wood and rocks and leather strings. I think it's jewelry.

Okay, well, I don't have much of a choice. I won't sleep on the floor, and the bed is big enough for two. Awkward? Maybe, but I'm past caring at this point. Here I am, stuck on an alien planet with no way to communicate my needs to this male, who took me into a forest a mile away to use a bathroom. The sooner I go to sleep, the sooner I can wake up the day after and find out that National Security has contacted these males and told them about the ship that blew up and about a pod that was never recovered.

To avoid revealing that they're predators, the males would say they have the lost girl, and boom, I'll be shipped back home.

I lie on my side.

He's stayed by the window.

I smile. "Good night."

He shows me his teeth, then rips off his kilt and pounces on me like an animal.

With a scream, I try rolling away, but he's on top of me, caging me in. I'm on my belly, cheek pressed to the bed, while his body touches mine, and he's hard. I mean he is *hard*, with a capital H. One hand presses my hip down, and he starts purring, the purr vibrating over my back and practically through my entire body.

I tense as he nips my earlobe and speaks through his purring, his thumb sliding back and forth over my jeans, inching toward my bare skin.

He purrs louder when he touches my hip, and just when I think he's about to tear off my pants, he turns on his side and takes me with him, balling up my body like a baby and practically encompassing all my surfaces with his own. He's a massive male, so he can cover me whole. I can't complain, because he's super warm, with fuzzy fur on his skin.

He seems to have settled in, and so has my heart after nearly beating out of my chest. My breathing slows as I listen to his purr and take comfort from the warmth of his body. His purr seems to relax me. I stare out the window, into the one light shining over my pod, wondering if I'll be leaving this place tomorrow. Or ever.

* * *

Something poking my shoulder awakens me. I open my eyes to the face of the alien male I slept with last night. Brain still coming around, I blink, wondering why he's crouching beside the bed and staring at me. Not wanting to be rude, I say, "Good morning."

"Good morning," he replies.

Wide awake and hopeful, I sit up in bed. "I understand you."

"And I you." He stands. Naked. With his long, wide shaft hanging down to midthigh. There's a…a small, unidentified body part at the top of his mushroom tip. I want to take a closer look, but find the flowers more appropriate at this time.

They withered. Not yet dead, but slowly dying. This bothers me more than it should. "You installed the translator while I slept?" I ask.

"I did."

"Could've woken me up."

"You seemed to need sleep. It is past the middle of the day."

True. I did sleep well.

I head for the bathroom, then realize there is no bathroom, and my brain can't process much of anything, let alone the thing at the tip of his cock, with no coffee. I scrub my face. "I feel like I slept for days."

"What is a day?"

"Twenty-four hours."

He shakes his head.

I frown. "Time spent in sunlight?"

"A span. Your species is nocturnal?"

"No."

"Then why do you feel you slept for days if you don't sleep during the time spent in sunlight?"

I laugh. "Good point. It's just something we say."

"We?"

Okay, okay, I can do this even with no coffee, yesterday's clothes, and faced with naked alien hotness. Here we go. I approach his massive muscular shape without looking at the ripped abs or how well hung he is, and concentrate on his face, how his mouth is plush, his nose kind of wider than an average man's, and his eyes bigger and white and a little scary. I extend a hand. "Stephanie. Representing womankind. What's your name?" Your species, planet, world?

"Womankind," he repeats.

"We're humans. We hail from Earth and arrive in round pods, crashing onto alien lands all over the galaxy." I smile, but he doesn't find me funny. "Shake my hand. It's a way of greeting."

He clasps my hand and yanks me to him, then starts purring again. I wiggle, then stop because he's growing harder between his legs.

"There's only one way to greet a female on my land. It's not by shaking hands."

I'm pretty sure I understand what he means, and now kind of regret that he installed a translator. I existed in mild oblivion for a while there, and now he's giving me a wide awakening.

"You think we could talk about greetings after coffee, bathroom, bath, food, stuff like that?"

"Bathroom?"

Oh no, this is a nightmare. If they don't have plumbing, I need to leave this place pronto. "A private place where we waste."

"Ah. We also waste."

"Bonding over waste is kind of strange."

He smiles. "You are funny, womankind."

"It's Stephanie."

He pulls back his lips, baring his teeth, and makes an S sound.

I think he's trying to say my name. I show him the T sound made by moving my tongue up behind my teeth, and in turn, he sticks his tongue out and licks my face.

"I can't move my tongue in the same way, so I will make a name for you."

"Okay, that's fine." I won't be here long enough to suffer a new name. I like my name. "And you are?"

"Hart. Kai of my people."

"Like a king?"

"Yes. The Alpha male. The primary predator at the top of the food chain."

"Um, that's concerning."

"It should be, because you marked my territory." He releases me and starts pacing the room.

It makes me nervous, and I sit on the bed, tucking my hands under my thighs. I thought our first conversation was going well, but no, aliens are aliens, and a pair of aliens can't understand each other well even when we think we do. "How did I mark your territory?"

"You peed on my hunting grounds."

"Oh that. Oh no." I wave my hand in front me, noting that the white polish from the French manicure on my left forefinger has chipped off. "I wasn't marking anything. I just had to pee. You know, waste."

"You consider my territory a bathroom?"

"No, no." He's stopped pacing, and facing me, he's still naked, and I'm trying and failing to look everywhere besides between his legs. I can't do that! The floor. It's crafted in delicate golden lines merging with purples in places. Slick, thin, cursive, feminine lines.

"Does my fitness offend you?" he asks.

I snap my gaze his way, but it's incredibly difficult to

make eye contact when eyes don't have pupils. I never thought about how the iris and pupil make eye contact easier. "Not at all." His body is made for pleasuring a woman, and it makes me uncomfortable that I think he's sexy. On Earth, while we trade with aliens, civilians rarely see any of the species. Most aliens use the trading ports and hardly ever have the need to land on the surface and interact with us. We definitely don't sleep with them. It's taboo to think of another species in the way I'm thinking of him. But his cock is long and thick, and I'm thirty-one and single.

"I am annoyed you're refusing to assess me for breeding."

"Hm?"

He taps his temple. "Is the translator not working?"

"Oh, it's working."

"Then why do you appear confused?"

"Breeding is a strong word to wake up to. Do you think maybe we can share a cup of coffee?" Surely there's coffee around here. God, please let there be coffee.

The alien's eyes narrow. "So you crash into my hall, mark my territory, and refuse to assess me for breeding. Do you know what we do with aliens like you?"

"Besides breed?"

"Yes."

"Nah, I'm trying not to think about it."

"You don't have to think. I'll tell you. We consume them." He steps closer, and the warmth of him makes me want to rub my body against his rock-solid torso. It's furry. Covered with tiny hairs. Warm. And he purrs. I mean he purrrrrs. I'm horny again. What did he say? Ah yes, something about consuming me. "You won't consume me, or you would have already."

"Maybe I'll consume you later."

I look up to see he's smiling. I think the alien made a joke. Or at least I hope he did.

His nose works, and he says, "You need to bathe."

Heat crawls up my cheeks. I tame the nest at the back of my head. "Lead the way." I'm also trying not to think about the breeding part of the conversation, and will think about it later, after coffee, when my brain isn't so muddled by the naked alien with a cock that I know for a fact would rock my world.

The male moves away, and I sigh, relieved he's out of sight. It makes it easier for me not to stare at him. He swipes a hand over the air in front of him, and a space opens inside his chambers. The space shows a path to a waterfall hitting a lake out of which steam rises. There're flowers and trees everywhere, and even small animals. It's a fairy-tale land with a hot bath. He walks into this land and extends a hand. "Come bathe," he purrs.

I put my hand in his, and he leads me into this landscape. When I look back, the bedroom is still there, which means that his people move from place to place with spatial openings only they can navigate, because I can't even see them.

I open my mouth to ask how he's moving around this way when he nudges the small of my back. I inch toward the lake and touch the water. It's warm, maybe a touch hot for my taste, but not burning, and I want so badly to bathe if only so he doesn't bring it up again. Nobody wants to smell bad, and I bet his sense of smell is better than mine. Most aliens classified as predators hunt, and for hunting, they need enhanced senses.

Glancing behind me, I see him crossing his arms over his chest. "Bathe."

"I will. As soon you leave."

I'm pretty sure the hyena cackle made deep within his chest is laughter.

"I don't know if there's something wrong with our translators," he says, "or if you're gently refusing my advances, but rest assured, womankind, when I say I'm annoyed you're not assessing me for breeding, it doesn't mean I want to breed you or that I'm thinking about breeding you. It means I've already made a decision to act upon my assessment of you and all there's left for you to do is look upon me and say *yes, Alpha.*" When I open my mouth to protest, he lifts a palm, effectively silencing me. "Shhh."

I gape at his arrogance.

"Nothing you say will make me leave. Might as well quit arguing and bathe to reduce the odor."

"Oh my God! You asshole." I pick up a rock, think better of it, and throw it in the lake.

He tilts his head. "A violent herbivore. What a predicament. You're interesting." Then he walks forward and I walk back, and he smirks as our bodies connect again. If I step back, I'll fall into the lake, and he knows it. Asshole.

CHAPTER SEVEN

HART

Like cornered prey, the female with a name I can only pronounce in my head stays put so that our chests connect, making me purr louder. I like how her breasts that feed the young feel on my chest, how last night, everywhere I touched was plush, and how her body is cold, making it necessary for me to keep it warm. "You must bathe now."

"Give me some privacy, and I will."

"And if I don't?"

"Then you will have a stinky alien in your chambers for the rest of your day."

"But I will have her in my chambers."

The female groans. "You won't let up, will you?"

I shake my head.

The female reaches for the bottom of the cloth that covers the top of her body and removes it. The breast contraption follows. Thank you, Bera, that thing is off. It looked like armor, as if breasts need confinement and protection. They certainly do not. I like them better loose.

To improve my view, I step back. Stephanie's cheeks color red for the second time, and while I don't understand the physical change, I sense her discomfort with undressing in front of a male. Perhaps I can put her at ease. "Not to worry, female. I find you suitable for breeding and pleasing to my eyes."

"That's comforting."

"You're welcome. Continue with no coloring in the cheeks."

She chuckles and removes the rest of her dysfunctional clothing. For a species that wastes below, they make their lives much harder by designing clothes that cover the wasting spaces. We wear vertos. It's practically a curtain. Much more efficient.

She's ogling me now, assessing my fitness. Finally. I pull back my shoulders, and my dick jumps, hits my navel, and bounces. Semen leaks from the hook at the tip of my dick and trails down the length. There you go, female. It works.

Her face is bright red now, and the scent of…arousal reaches my nose. I inhale a lungful. My, my, my. I lick my lips, thinking of how I'm gonna mount this female when she goes into heat, then remember I still haven't established if she's a carnivore.

"You're looking at me like I'm something you wanna eat," she says.

"And your scent tells me you're looking at me like I'm something you wanna fuck. Do you?"

She covers her face. "You're too blunt. I can't do this." The female spins and dives into the water, and I watch her swim, wondering if she can breathe under it in a way my people can't. Soon, she comes up and gasps for air. Our species are similar in more ways than one. Even our physical appearance is similar, which makes me think our breeding will succeed, and we will be able to produce young. I walk along the baths, speaking over the noise the waterfall makes while hitting the rocks behind her.

She's more comfortable now, swimming, twirling.

"The beloys flower," I say and point to her right, "can be used for fragrance."

"I must really smell bad to you," she says but swims toward the flower.

"Not at all," I whisper, and silently slide into the water while my prey is distracted. By the time she realizes I'm at her side, it's too late. I cage her in, pressing my front to her back, and lick a place between her neck and shoulder, a place I want to bite to mark, but fear if I do, I'll lust for her flesh in ways I'd regret.

Eating and breeding, two primal instincts, war inside me. I scent a hearty meal that makes my mouth water, and I also smell her arousal that invites my advances. Most prey fear me, and I can smell it. If the prey fears me, I wanna eat it. But this one is aroused, so I wanna fuck. Still, she's prey, not an equal to me, and I haven't experienced this sort of struggle before. Here I have a prey animal I want to breed. An oxymoron. Hunger for her flesh has a new meaning, and I want to investigate.

"I need to taste between your legs," I say, then drag my tongue over the soft skin between her shoulder blades. "I know you want me to." I grab her hips and lift her over the edge so she lies on her belly. The place between her legs appears in front of me. Her buttocks are spectacular, the softest part of her body. I grab one cheek and wiggle it, noticing she's watching me over her shoulder. The scent of fear enters my nose as I climb over her body, holding myself up so I appear as if I will mount her now.

Her arousal intensifies, but so does the smell of fear. The way she responds to me only makes me war with my instincts even more. "I'm not going to hurt you. We already established that. Try to curb your fear."

The female nods, and for the first time since I've met her,

she's not talking back. I don't know what to make of it, but I like it. I peck her rosy cheek. Her body's much warmer now. "Don't fear me. All I'm gonna do is lick between your legs. It's how I can show you my interest and also how I can taste your arousal. Some of it tells me if we're compatible. You can resist if you like, though that will make me want it more, and since I'm the Kai, I get what I want. Today, tomorrow, whenever." I rest my dick on her bottom, make it twitch, then inhale to gauge how she feels about that.

Stephanie swallows. I can see she's uncertain, and the threat of her rejection crackles in the sky like a thunderbolt, threatening to disrupt my advances, and I can't let it. I just have to try harder, entice her more. I slip a finger between her butt cheeks and feel a small hole first, then a bigger hole, a wet one, telling me her body has already slickened her channel for penetration. I swipe back and forth over her slit, drawing out more of her liquid, until her arousal blossoms in the air, drowning the scent of the otherwise potent beloys flower.

Her eyes close, and I slide down her body, then stick my tongue out and spread her globes. What's there is unlike anything I've seen before. There are two holes, one smaller, one bigger, and since I don't know the significance of the other hole, I stick with my instincts and swipe my tongue over the place that's wetter than the other, the place I scented when she ran to me, the same place that made me question my instinct to eat her.

I taste and finally understand why I didn't consume her.

It's because this place produces a potent and sweet taste on my tongue, and the more I lick, the more I want it. It's almost addictive, and soon, I learn that savoring the liquid like this makes the alien pussy give me more of it, and so I bury my entire face between her globes and purr my lungs out when she starts moaning.

I tune in to the sounds she makes. They're of pleasure, not pain, so I'm doing great. I lap at her hole and reach for my cock, stroking it while I lick her, imagining mounting her like this over the ground, extending my hook in search of her womb and dropping my seed inside her. The images make me stroke myself faster, and my cock grows, the hook ready to attach on her womb, when I sense a bump under my tongue.

I flick the bump, and the female pushes back against my face.

The bump is a go. Growling, I flick it again, and she pushes back some more, practically suffocating me. I hold my breath and dive inside there, licking only over the bump and hearing her moaning louder than before. I stroke my cock, sensing my balls filling, drawing up, and the hook hardening like a thorn, searching for a womb. I fist the top of my cock and prevent the hook from ejecting my seed. It's painful, and I growl while licking her.

Stephanie arches her back, her body locks, and liquid gushes out of the hole and onto my tongue. Stunned that a female species can ejaculate, I get drunk on the fluid, fighting her legs from closing, but alas, Stephanie slides down into the lake, bumping her bottom on my cock.

I purr at her ear. "Are you inviting me to mount you?"

She turns, her face as red as a tomtac plant. "No."

I lift her up a bit so I don't have to bend, and I press my lips over hers. She doesn't respond.

"Do your people kiss?" I ask.

"Yes."

"Do you?"

"Sometimes."

"How about now so I can finally pit my tongue against yours? See whose tongue is more agile." The goddesses gave me a tongue so I can lick this female's pussy. Of course. What other purpose would a seldom-used muscle have?

I don't wait for an answer, but kiss her softly and purr even more softly, allowing me to lull her, make her feel more comfortable, less resisting, just the way prey should be. Soft, pretty, cute, and submissive, bending to my will, and my will is to breed, preferably right now. I fist my cock. "Are you sure you're not inviting me to mount you?"

Against my lips, her mouth stretches into a smile. "I'm sure."

"Is it because you find me unfit for breeding? I assure you I'm fit. Let me show you."

Stephanie presses a hand over my chest, and I grab it, peeling it off my chest and directing it down so she can get a feel for my fitness.

"Hart." I hear Mas's voice in my chambers. Gonna ignore him. I'm having a moment with my...female.

I run her palm over my cock.

"It's smooth," I say. "I don't have two of these to fill your two holes but I promise one will be memorable."

Her eyes widen. "Oh no, the other hole is...inaccessible."

"According to whom?"

"Me, primarily."

"I can be persuasive."

"I've noticed."

I kiss her mouth again. "I want to make out with your other lips."

She pulls back and balls her hand into a fist. "I want to bathe and use this nice-smelling flower on my hair and body. Are there more flowers like this one? For the body and hair?"

"Hart, answer me," comes from the chambers.

I ignore Mas's voice. "There are. What is your fascination with flowers?"

"They're pretty. Looking at them makes me happy."

She's sharing secrets I can leverage. I don't believe she realizes she's delivering valuable information that I can and will use to win the games, and I know there will be games. Herbivore or not, she tastes like a breeder to me, and by now, most males would have figured out my keeping her isn't about food. One part of wining the games is beating the other males. The second part is winning the female. "I will get you more flowers."

"A vase will do for the ones I already picked."

"What is a vase?"

"A bowl with water one can put flowers in."

I purse my lips, thinking of bowls and where I'm gonna find them. How strange.

"Hookhead!" Mas shouts. "The males are ready, and you know the rules."

I leap out of the water, shaking the droplets off my body. "Come," I say to Stephanie.

"Where?"

"Back inside."

"But I haven't bathed."

"You have. The water has cleansed your body. No time for fragrance now. Come."

The female makes an effort to climb out to the surface, and I have to say, this alien species appears uncoordinated. I want to haul her up so she doesn't have to expend the effort she's expending, but I'm fascinated with how her limbs bend in slow, jerky movements. It all seems awkward to me.

Standing, she tries wiping the dirt off her hands and knees, but smears it all over instead. She sighs. "I'm dirty again."

"That's because you're crawling over mud." Why would anyone do that after a bath? What is wrong with this species?

"I had to climb out."

"Why climb when you can leap?"

"Um, I can't jump the way you can."

"I know that. But can't you jump at all?"

"Sure." She bounces in place. "There, I jumped."

She must be joking again. I crouch and jump across the bath, landing before my chambers. "Your turn. Come on." While I know predators are more agile than prey, she must at least be able to jump a little higher than what she showed me.

I expect her to follow, but Stephanie bends and scoops up some water to clean herself again, then rounds the entire bath, and by the time she reaches me, I'm thinking this female might be at the very bottom of our food chain, and that's dangerous.

"It's okay," I tell her, although I worry about her. "I'm plenty fast and agile enough for both of us."

"Where are you going?"

"We are going to the Hall of the Fallen."

"And once there?"

"You'll meet the other contestants."

"What do you mean?"

"We're opening the games." Bera delivered a breeder. Or Amti, in which case, I'm mad and lusting over an herbivore, and my instincts can't be trusted. And yet, I can't ignore either goddess or refuse the gift they bestowed upon us.

"What games?"

"The courting games." I shake the water from my hair. Why is she not shaking the water off hers? Maybe it doesn't bother her the way it bothers me, but it should. With her body temperature being lower, she should remove the droplets before she gets too cold.

"What's that mean?" Stephanie asks and hugs herself.

See? She's cold. *Shake off the damn water,* I want to order her. What in Herea's name is going on here? "It means the males will compete for the right to breed you."

"You're not the only one who wants to breed me?"

45

"I am not, but I will be the only one who does." She appears surprised we're going to compete for the right to breed her. I haven't a clue how the males of her kind go about obtaining breeding rights to females, but this is how it's done in the tribal lands. The moment I refused to consume her, and when the word of her marking the forest spread—I have my brother to thank for that—my males decided to ambush me about her as I made my way back with a translator.

They want to breed a female too.

They want a partner to warm their beds. Or keep them cold, in the case of this alien species.

They want a gentle touch.

We want what all males of the galaxy want: to protect and procreate, and those instincts war with our predatory instincts, the ones that tell us everyone we encounter is food. But with her arrival, I have a chance to not just beat the other males in the games, but also to beat my own instincts and perhaps even renew our faith in the goddesses I thought had deserted us. With no females left after the wars, what I saw in the eyes of my males was the hope this alien gave them, and I won't squander it.

Also, I won't lose.

CHAPTER EIGHT

STEPHANIE

Hart has a way with his mouth. Not just the way he kisses or eats pussy.

It's the words he forms with that mouth, the persuasive way he articulates language, and I'm thinking I probably would've been better off with no translator. He talks the talk and walks the walk and definitely knows how to command a female. His body is my erotic dream, albeit a little strange and definitely plenty crazy considering he's a male of a different species.

I rub my shoulders, looking around for a closet or something where he stores his clothes. Or, say, a towel while Hart fastens a short black leather kilt over his middle and straps on his weapons. Where were those clothes? Things just appear as if by magic.

"Where did you get the kilt?"

"The what?"

I point. "Things seem magical around here."

He slides me a gaze and smirks. "It's a verto. Only my dick is magical."

"You have to stop that."

"Which that?"

"The blatant flirting." I'm sure I'm blushing again.

"I don't know how to talk any other way. Molding words and mincing them creates confusion and makes my males feel lost because they have to translate what I'm trying to say. I'd rather just go on and say it. For example, I'd love to keep you here naked and barefoot."

"I imagine you would, caveman."

"Cavemen isn't translating. You'll explain later." He purses his lips. "It has just occurred to me I have no idea where to procure clothes for a female."

"What do you mean?"

"There are no females. So no clothes."

"Oh. Ooooo." Oh shit. That can't be right. It must be the translator. "How did you come to be?"

"Long story. Save that for later too. Provide me suggestions for clothing now."

"Clothes for boys will do."

He smiles a sad smile. "No females. No young."

I'm trying to process the underlying message. His people are all grown males, which means stagnant, which means they'll go extinct soon, which makes me a hot commodity they're willing to compete for. It also means this male won't send me back home or even think of sending me back. He's going to breed me and keep me. It all kind of crashes down on me, and I sit on the bed, staring ahead. "Oh my God, I'm never leaving this place."

Someone please pass me a paper bag. My chest starts hurting, breaths coming out in short pants, and I try some anxiety breathing exercises I've learned during my allotted Home Entertainment time. It doesn't work, and when I start sounding like a freaked-out ape, I close my mouth and breathe through my nose.

Hart crouches in front of me, face grim. "What awkward

thing is happening with you right now?" He sniffs, nose turned up, wiggling. "You're under duress. Do not worry about a single thing. I will take care of you. Whatever it is you need. Besides coffee. And for now, besides clothes. Minor things. The major thing is waiting for you upstairs."

"I'm never leaving this planet."

"That's right." He pats my head. "It's nicer here anyway."

"How do you know?"

"Your transport system stored a few images of Earth. Dominated by water creatures, little land. Leads me to believe you have scarce resources that are becoming scarcer and driving the need for your species to find other habitats like Mars, a completely artificial habitat. Also, I saw one of the mankind. He covered his entire body, which makes it impossible for a female to assess him for breeding. You will be pleased with the selection upstairs even if you don't consider any of them."

"I'm not participating in your games."

His face hardens, and he stands. "You are, female."

"I'm *not*. I want to go home." I want to cry, but I won't. I'll cry when I'm alone. Oh my God, I'm never leaving this place. I don't know what to do about it. I don't know how to deal with it.

"Why do you want to go home?"

"Because... because..." I frown. Over the years, the five largest corporations have moved to Mars, taking their resources and jobs with them while billions of us on Earth mainly work to qualify for jobs on Mars. The move to Mars came with a natural human desire for independence and more adventure as well as advancement.

Recently, leaders emerged, ones who want Mars to become a separate entity from Earth. Currently, our media is in an uproar. People fear one of the warrior classes of aliens will align with the billionaires on Mars and stop defending the Earth from the aliens who would love to conquer us. While it's unlikely something terrible will happen, it's not impossible.

Mom's already on Mars. She married one of the billionaires with his own kids. He prefers I stay away, and he's got her all wrapped up in money and prestige. I never knew my dad. What's at home that makes me wanna go back? A job at the IT company where I stare at the screen all day and interpret numbers? I'm shit with spreadsheets and data, but the job pays well, so I grind daily. I don't have a boyfriend. I don't even have a cat. Mira is my only friend, and I'll miss her. I'll also miss... I know what. "Familiarity," I tell him. "Independence. Freedom to move around whenever I want and wherever I want."

"And coffee?"

"That too."

He crouches again, puts a hand on my knee, and squeezes. "As the spans roll, as you spend more time here and with me, I and all the tribal land that's mine will become familiar. You have independent thoughts. Those are yours, and nobody can take them from you. Freedom to move around will also come with time. Don't despair."

I can't be seen as a weakling or have a breakdown in front of this strong and hard male, and in any case, it would do me no good. I nod.

"Are you done despairing now?" He leans in, waiting for an answer. Tattoos curve around his jaw. They're stunning. He's stunning. I want to reach out and trace the lines over his jaw, but I nod again, telling him I'm done despairing even when I'm not.

"I'm desperate to dress you in something. I can't have dozens of males staring at the prize. They'll have to earn that privilege, and I'm not gonna let them earn it."

"Because you're gonna win."

"In my head, I already won. Though I will attempt to stop the games, my males deserve hope, and the games raise our spirits. We love the games and haven't held them in...well, since the Ra slayed my parents."

Banging rings from upstairs, and the roof starts shaking. I look up. "What's going on?"

I expect him to say earthquake, but he chuckles. "Males stomping in the hall. Getting impatient with my delay. Next move for them is to force their way down here."

"And you don't want that."

"No."

"So I have to dress."

"Yes."

"Do you have a closet? A place where you keep your clothes?"

"I do. Would you like to wear something of mine?"

"Do I have a choice?"

He adopts this funny look that I can't quite read and moves to the side of the bed, where a space opens and clothes on a rack appear. He sifts through outfits by moving his finger in front of him while outfits spin one after the other before him. This is some great tech, and while we have similar stuff on Earth, we don't have these special openings we can call upon at will.

A fur coat with cut-off arms appears, and he brings it to me. I push my hands into it and fasten it in the front. It hangs to my knees. "This will do. Thank you."

Hart sits on the throne and extends a hand.

I take it and he pulls me so I fall into his lap. He fists my hair and kisses me. "Do not be afraid. You're a prize, remember? Nobody will hurt you."

"Got it."

"Also, if you look at any other male besides me, I'll kill them in the games." The throne lifts and travels upward slowly. I get the feeling Hart doesn't want us to emerge upstairs, which makes me more nervous.

"Keep your eyes on the floor as you did when I tried to show you my fitness."

"No problem." He calls his body with that monster cock his fitness and thinks I can resist looking at it. Oh Lord, have mercy on me when he figures out I have zero resistance when he takes off his clothes. Zero. But hey, I'm keeping up a brave front.

Before the disk emerges upstairs, I feel the energy in the hall. They're still drumming on the floor, urging Hart to come up, and when the throne ascends and locks into place, they stop and stand at attention. Hart lifts me out of his lap, and as I stand, he fists my hair and kisses me again.

The males boo him, and he growls, then releases me. "Sit. Eyes on the floor."

I bark like a Yorkie.

His eyes widen, and I shake my head and sit down, cross one leg over the other, and look at what's in front of me. A huge space packed with massive males wearing kilts and ancient weapons. Through the open door, I see more males filling the bridge. Surely, they're not all here for the games or the prize (me). Surely, most are spectators. My heart thumps in my ears, and I think I might faint when they start painting various tribal symbols on their faces and bodies, reminding me of Viking legends and their warrior rituals before battle.

On my right, a male with long, light, almost blond hair, approaches Hart and stretches out a cupped palm, ink dripping between his fingers. Hart dips two fingers in the black ink and looks over his shoulder. Gaze locked with mine, he brings two fingers to his throat, draws a line, then lightly touches his lips. He can make a simple translator signal look sexy. A drop of ink drips from his bottom lip and onto his chin, making a line as it slides down. Butterflies stir in my belly as his gaze stays on me, and I realize I could watch him forever. He's sexy, hard, and forbidden, and I feel rebellious for acknowledging our intimacy.

The male with the ink approaches me and offers me his cupped hand. I dip a finger into the ink and bring it to my nose first. It smells like burned charcoal. Strange, but when in Rome... I draw a line on my throat and touch my lips.

The male stands beside me and snorts. "The Kai has a clear advantage."

The males boo, but one says, "Not if he's dead."

"Who said that?" Hart asks. When nobody steps forward, he steps down and elbows his way through the males to find the culprit, leaning against the door. He's painted one entire side of his face, the side with an eye that shows the slit pupil and silver iris. His other eye is like everyone else's: white.

"Ark." Hart touches his cheek to the male's cheek and smears some of the ink onto his face. "When did you arrive?"

"Yesterday."

"Why haven't you come to me?"

"And give away my surprise? My friend, I was preparing traps for you for the games. Something I hear you haven't done." He steps to the side, and Hart's jaw hardens at the same time as the new male winks at me.

I don't wink back. I don't like him. What kinds of traps has he prepared? Better the monster I know than the one I don't. Not that I know Hart, but the reason I'm alive is because he hasn't consumed me. I can't say the others, who attacked the second I landed, would show the same restraint.

Hart snorts. "I don't need traps to beat you all."

Shouting commences.

The male who stands next to me touches the throne's armrest, then proceeds to move his hand in the space before him. I stand next to him to see what he's doing, and while I can tell he's looking at something, I can't see what it is.

"The turnout is bigger than I expected." He glances at me. "Maybe I should enter. One more slot left before I close the games. What do you think, female? Wanna experience the fuck of your lifetime?"

The arrogance on this one. What a dick. "Eat me, asshole," I mumble, then sit back on the throne and fix the fur over my thigh, trying to yank it a little down to cover more of my leg. When it won't stretch—obviously—I huff and give up. Looking up, I notice the hall has quieted, and they're all staring. I clear my throat, and look to Hart for answers.

"Eat me? Be careful what you wish for, female," Hart says, diverting their attention from what I said in a room full of predators. *Smart. Real smart, Stephanie.* My mouth's gonna cost me my life if any of these males decide I'll make a great meal.

Hart stares out the windows overlooking his land. I stand back up again and walk to the windows on this side of the throne, taking care I don't leave the upper part of the hall, meaning I don't walk down those steps. I've noticed none of the males climbed them.

Pockets of different landscapes appear and disappear before my eyes. They're flashes, appearing out of thin air, lingering for few seconds, then disappearing, only to be replaced by another flash, but never exactly in the same place.

"What is all this?" I ask.

"Mas will explain," Hart says. "Won't you, Mas?"

"Not really. Today's winner can explain when he wins the night with her."

"They're competing for a night with me?"

"Mm-hm," Hart says.

"So it's over tonight?"

Mas sighs, and I turn, waiting for an explanation. He graces me with a glance, finally making eye contact and acknowledging me as a person. "Four hundred males. Three days. Two nights. One winner. The prize? You." He makes a fist and strikes the air before him. The windows burst open, and the males leap out of them, snarling and gnawing at each other. I scream, rushing to hide behind the throne as I did when I first got here.

When I hear silence and I'm sure they left the hall, I stand back up and round the throne.

The only one standing there is Hart. "I'll see you tonight," he says.

"Keep stalling, love bug," Mas says, fingers flying over thin air, "and you'll come crying to me when you lose."

With a powerful thrust, he hops onto the windowsill. The shifting of muscle, like water rushing under ice, signals his dual form. He snarls and leaps out. I rush to the window to follow his leap and see he's landed on top of one male and has crushed him to the ground. I gasp, shocked.

"Are the games fought to the death?" I ask Mas.

"It depends."

"On what?"

"On the threat," Mas answers from right behind me. Fear makes me freeze. He purrs. "I smell your fear, you know. Such a delicate scent. I don't know if it makes me want to eat you or fuck you."

I ball up my fists. "I'm the prize. If you want to eat me or fuck me, you have to play in the games." I spin and look up, forcing myself to lock eyes with his. "You didn't enter, so stay away from me."

He smirks, still too close for comfort but I can't back away or back down. Shorter than Hart, but still broad and solid, he's got the menacing orange eyes of a predator hiding behind the male, and he makes me uneasy.

My stomach growls in a loud protest of hunger.

Mas narrows his eyes. "Don't get growly with me, alien."

I press a hand over my stomach, wanting to tell him how hungry I am, but deciding I don't want to tell him anything because I don't like him. Actually, I don't find him as safe as I find Hart. Hart won't hurt me. I'm unsure about this one, though he seems to be trusted with me since we're alone.

"Are you safeguarding me? Is that why you can't enter?" I ask.

Mas continues moving his hand over the space before him.

"That's it. You can't hurt me and nobody else can either because you're…you're…like a designated something."

"A guardian."

"Ha!"

A small smile plays over his lips. "Don't let it go to your head, female. Four hundred males competing is enough for a girl's ego, no?"

I chuckle. "True that."

"You don't seem to be interested in watching the games. Why?"

"I am interested." But also a bit light-headed and hungry. And decaffeinated. My belly growls again. It's so empty. I hope Hart brings back some food.

CHAPTER NINE

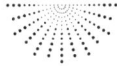

HART

Day one in the games is always the biggest rush, especially since we haven't held games in the history of my tribal leadership, which says I haven't secured a future for my people yet, and they won't pass up a once-in-a-lifetime chance not only to compete with each other, but also to secure a possible breeder, one that, if carnivorous, would deliver healthy, living, breathing young.

The nipples on her breasts tell me that's a real possibility. Our young feed on breast milk too.

However, along with fortune comes misfortune.

Ark, the Ra tribal leader, has entered as well. Not too long ago, we signed a truce, one his father would never have agreed to. Ark wants peace. I want peace. But we also have a history of war between our two tribes, enough bloodshed, revenge, and pillaging that could get brought up at any moment during the games and cause yet another conflict. I'm certain he's not alone, and I'm certain he didn't lie about the traps he set for me.

I pretend he's welcome on my land.

He pretends we are friends.

Since there's only a little over a thousand Ka males left, avoiding the games would've been ideal. But if I did, they'd call me a coward, and challenges would mount daily until they exhausted and killed me, in which case Ark would take advantage of our leadership vacuum.

Preserving my males is my priority, especially since we have a blood-hungry Ra in the west constantly trying to find new ways to kill us off. Ark showing up for the games is nothing short of shocking. Still, I'm gonna win.

The games started at four hundred males. As we entered the portals, we're already down to about half of that number as some males entered portals Mas designed as dead ends, traps, paths leading to nowhere, and could cost a male the game if he got stuck inside with no way out.

On day one, the goal is to get the breeder a gift of her choosing. She accepts the gift and thereby invites the winning male to mount her.

Indeed, I have the upper hand.

I know she collects flowers and wants a bowl, a pottery thing of some sort or another. My people hunt for food and we have no need for such things, but as I run over yet another male, avoiding crushing his leg in the process, I twist another's arm, push him, and enter the hunting grounds before he does. I stop by the portal control facing Sor, a male I hunt with often.

He's keeping the portal open, letting males inside when he should close it so we have fewer competitors on the grounds.

"Close the portal, Sor."

"Stay back, or I'll collapse it."

"Close the fucking portal. What are you doing?"

Two of his brothers enter, and he closes the portal. They form a circle around me. More males rise from behind the bushes, and even more drop from the trees.

I take stock of my position. "A Karni Ambush? You fucking pussies." A Karni Ambush is a tactic used by weaker males to defeat a stronger male who is most likely to win. They band together and form a subtribe, then attack the stronger male, who often capitulates to prevent death. Once the largest threat is eliminated, the males in the subtribe outplay each other. "This game can't be fought to the death," I remind them. "There are thirteen of you, and I'm not exiting the game, so before you rush me, think hard. I will win."

Sor's brother Riv steps forward. He doesn't reach for his weapons, and his hunting form holds steady. He wants to talk.

"You've allowed the Ra tribe's Alpha to compete," he says.

"I have."

"You broke our tribal laws. The enemy can't compete."

"We signed a treaty with them, or did you forget?"

He thumps his chest. "I forget nothing." He points. "You forgot they slaughtered our villages, took everything from us."

Old wounds die hard. "I made a decision, and you can either fall in line or leave the tribe." I turn my back to him, confident he won't attack. It is cowardly, and he's not a coward. None of them are. My heart breaks that they've chosen to rally against me instead of against the Ra Alpha, but I see the logic. I have the best chance of winning, and so I must be eliminated.

The three males standing in my way part for me, and I make sure I brush Sor's shoulder as I walk past him, whispering, "Leave the game."

"Aimea will come for you," he says. Aimea is a divine bringer of doom.

I stop beside him to look him in the eye. "You're wrong. Aimea will come for us all if we war with the Ra again." That said, I go about my gift hunt, alert for the ambush I know is coming, wondering if they want to wound me or kill me.

* * *

I stand before two trees, debating which of the two types of wood would make a sturdy and aesthetically pleasing bowl. The aged bark of the oke tree indicates it had matured and the wood would last long, but it's also almost impossible to carve and paint, which means I can't do either. It would make a plain, boring bowl.

The fila tree's wood retains ink better, but it's less sturdy than the oke tree. Hmm.

Somewhere behind me, the subtribe is closing in. They've been following me. Turning, I snarl, my hunter pushing against my skin, wanting to tear them all to pieces. But I can't. The Ra Alpha entered the competition, and if he decides to raise hell, I want more of my males with me and after him and whomever he brought with him.

Fucking treaties. I hate peace. But I hate the wars that have killed my males and all our females more. Making bowls, competing, and courting females is more fun. If only I knew how to make bowls and court females. I don't, but I have to learn while fending off the pack.

I glance up into the branches of the fila tree. I leap and jab my claws into the tree trunk, then hop over a thick branch. Before I take out my ax, I survey the grounds and spot a brown paw hiding behind the bush not too far from me. I can't tell who it is, but he's a bold male to come this close alone. Maybe he wants to die. I lick my lips, already feeling his blood on my tongue, my hunter clawing at my brain. *No, no, can't do that.* Pain shoots up my spine as I rein in the killer instincts.

Back to courting, gifting, competing. I test the thick

branch I'm standing on to make sure it's gonna hold me and walk over to a thinner branch, then chop it off and walk back. Sitting down, I lean back on the trunk, alert to my surroundings while reshaping the wood with a dagger. When I have a nice round piece, all I have to do is dig a hole in it. I jab the dagger into the core and twist. A tiny piece chips off. I keep jabbing, digging, twisting the dagger in the wood.

At this rate, I'll take a span and another span to polish it, paint it, carve it, make it beautiful. I don't have that kind of time, but I do what I can with the time I have. I keep digging, chipped pieces falling to the ground.

Night approaches, and the forest comes alive with hoots and warbles of nocturnal creatures. I'm still at it, progressing, but slowly, and the deadline looms. She could've already accepted a gift from someone else. Someone could've stolen her and run off. Mas could've tried to double-cross me. Where is my brother? Did he snag her just to spite me? Maybe she ran off.

Paranoia about my female raises the hair at the back of my neck, makes my lip curl up. *Why did I leave Mas around her while I'm not?* The thought of losing her grips me and won't let go. Snarling, I holster the dagger and toss the ugly bowl. I'm out of time and out my of mind.

A branch cracks. The pack decided to close in.

"I'm in the foulest of moods," I say. "Stay back."

I drop from the branch and land lightly on the ground, trying to think of what else I could bring her that she would accept over all other things two hundred males will bring her. Why, oh why can't I kill every male on the planet? It would be so much easier than carving bowls.

I stare at the wet ground, then up the fila tree, where beautiful flowers in every color in the land hang from the branches, their petals shy and cute. Submissive. They remind me of her. My female collects them because looking at them makes her happy. Why make a bowl, pick flowers, and do all that when I can bring her the entire tree? Brilliant.

On all fours, in hunter, I flex my claws, and get to digging around the base of the trunk, my claws ripping through roots, throwing dirt everywhere, sinking deeper and deeper into the hole I dig up around the tree, so when they jump me, I'm in a bad position.

Five pack males land on me, biting, clawing, tearing off chunks of my flesh and snapping their teeth near my jugular. Jugular targeting is intended to kill. None of them are playing a game. They're not gonna wound me, they're trying kill me. So be it.

I bite Sor's belly. His blood spills over my tongue, his squeak making me tear into him with my claws. Once a hunter tastes blood, it's over. Sparing them is no longer an option. They've cornered me down here, attacking me on all sides, aiming solely for my throat. I'm biting back while guarding my neck and belly when I see a white-and-gray hunter with bright silver eyes jump into the fray.

It's the Ra Alpha, and we lock eyes and, as hunters, an understanding passes between us. He wants to kill. I want to kill. And so we do. He takes two in the back. I take three in the front and chew through them, crushing bones, ripping flesh, severing jugulars, tearing their cheeks from their faces. It's over in a matter of minutes, and I pant, surveying the carnage, eyeing the Alpha hunter across from me.

He shakes his head.

He knows what I'm thinking. I want to continue. I want to tear into him.

I lean forward, growling, readying to spring at him when he surprises me and lowers his head, showing my hunter submission.

Before I risk a war, I force myself to change back into a male. As my brain returns to a more rational state, I take account of the carnage. Inside my chest, my heart hurts. When the taste of blood lands on our hunters' tongues, my people go into a frenzy, a berserk state of mind, and until all challengers have been killed, we don't come out of it. At least not easily. My knees fold, and I kneel beside Sor's torn body.

All our lives, we train to rein in our killer instincts and repress them so we can take control of our senses, and most times, we succeed. It has taken a single alien female to turn my world upside down and send me into a frenzy.

Ark sits on the other side, his hunter's gaze on me. From his chest, he growls low, and I know he's trying to rein in his hunter. Once neatly braided gray-and-white hair curtains his face, blood dripping onto his lap as he shuffles his feet, preparing to pounce.

I growl a warning, and speak, my words mangled as they rumble from my chest. "I'm hanging on to sanity by a thread here, Ark. Relax."

He wipes his mouth, then his hands on a black ierto, the one-piece leather garment the Ra wear. "I had nothing to do with this," he says and leans back against the tree.

I snort. "I don't believe you, and I didn't need your help."

He smirks. "But I stepped in anyway. Show of solidarity, yeah?"

"Fuck you. I owe you nothing, and you enjoyed killing my males."

Ark smiles. "I followed some of these males here. They traveled for the games from my borders."

"So?"

He picks up the hem of his ierto to wipe his face. "They were on patrol and met with some of my males, including Gur. Perhaps you've heard of him?"

"The one who wouldn't sign the treaty?" Ark forced Gur's hand on the treaty. Feeling my hunter settle, my chest hurts, and I mourn my kaiens, these five tribal warriors under my protection who swore loyalty to me but then attacked me.

"That's the one."

"What's he doing on my border?"

"I promised him land so he'd sign the treaty."

While Ark is an Alpha hunter of the Ra tribe, he's not a Rai. The Ra have no one leader. Each earl decides for himself and his earliens, the warriors under his protection. "You made him an earl," I conclude. "And is that the land he wanted, or is it the land you gave him?"

"I need my tribe united like yours is."

He evaded my question. I don't press. "You're the least united tribe on the planet."

He chuckles. "I'm not the one being targeted."

"True." I nod. "Go on. You're in a chatty mood."

"Gur must've turned them and sent them after you. The games were just an excuse, an opportunity to kill with no consequences. You did the right thing."

"Killing my males is never the right thing. Certainly not when I'm not in a position to easily replace them." He knows our numbers, and there's no sense in lying. I wipe my bloody face on my arm. "Besides, I don't think it was Gur."

He points at my dead hunters. "I've been watching Gur, and I tracked these two males from the borders."

"Maybe they really want the female," I say. "You can't presume breeding isn't motivation to kill."

Ark snorts. "She's cute, but not that cute."

I rise. "Watch your mouth."

He wags his eyebrows, his hunter still watching me with cruel silver eyes. "Don't you want to hear how she got here?"

I tilt my head. "Your warbird had something to do with it."

"Mmhm."

"Something went wrong, then?"

"On the contrary. Everything is going just right."

I narrow my eyes. He's up to something.

He lifts his palms. "I'm innocent."

Rolling my eyes, I hop out of the hole I dug and stare down at the mangled bodies.

Ark leaps out too, landing across from me. "Gur will compromise the treaty."

"How?"

"He has a human female, and when he announces the games and your males come, he'll kill them all."

"Not if one of them wins."

"He has no intention to play fair or hand over the female. He'll kill her before he lets your tribe breed her."

"This is why you came for my games. To see if I'd let you compete and win. To see if I'd try to kill you."

Another nod.

I run my hand through my hair. It comes away bloody, and I go to wipe on my kilt, but it's bloody too. As are my chest and thighs. I'm covered in the red blood of my males. "He's not my male. Take care of him."

Ark scrubs his jaw. "I was hoping you'd take care of Gur for me."

I cross my arms over my chest. "Why would I do that?"

"Because I can deliver more human females."

"I only need the one I'm competing for, and she's already here."

"Why only one when there're billions of them."

Billions. *Billions!* He's promising my tribe breeders, which means survival, greater numbers of hunters, stronger armies, stronger tribe. "Can they give us young?" I ask. Young that lives and breathes, but I don't say that. I don't have to. He knows the stakes. He knows we're all gonna die if we keep doing what we've been doing.

"That's what you're gonna find out. Unless you want me to find out." He winks.

I grit my teeth.

"I have to ask," he says. "What the fuck were you doing down there?"

"Digging up a tree."

He blinks. "Why?"

"Because the tree will make her happy." I smile. "Bet you didn't think of that."

"Only because I am sane." Ark spins on his heel and walks away.

"Wait. I can't carry a tree on my own and make it there on time."

He's walking back to the portal exit.

"Hey!"

Ark disappears into the forest. I look down into the pit of flesh and bone. If I can't deliver the gift I wanted to deliver to her, the very least I can do is give my males a warning. I dive back in there and pick up a piece of Sor.

CHAPTER TEN

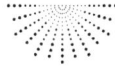

STEPHANIE

The males returned in fewer numbers than when they started, but still, they returned with gifts they laid on the steps of the throne. Most of them came back unscathed, but some sport gashes on their bodies. More than half, obviously, didn't come back at all.

They've retreated into groups. Some linger inside the hall, some outside on the bridge. Hart hasn't returned, and in order to make the first night of the games count, he has to present me with a gift before nightfall.

I stand at the window, glancing at the setting sun, wanting to chew my nails again. Meanwhile, Mas is building a fire in the middle of the hall. The rising smoke draws the males, and they seem content inhaling it. It seems to relax them.

I'm hungry, thirsty, and tired, but most of all apprehensive. Their Kai is running late, and he doesn't strike me as the type to be late. I worry something happened to him, and he'll get replaced. Better the monster I know. At least Hart kept me warm at night and didn't let me sleep on the freezing floor. He didn't violate me or kill me.

A commotion draws my attention. A male appears at the entrance holding something in his hand. It's another gift. Mas asked that I honor their traditions and show each of them respect upon completion of the task. I walk back to the throne to stand before it again as I have countless times tonight so that Ark, the Alpha of a rival tribe, Ra, can present his gift. Mas briefed me on some of the brutal history as well as told me this is not just any hall, it is the Hall of the Fallen, equivalent to a cathedral, a place of worship where no violence is allowed.

Blood stains Ark's kilt, and before he presents a gift, he picks a bit of flesh from between his teeth and spits it on the floor. The other Ka males crowd him, growling, their hunter bodies moving under their skin, signaling impending violence. My heart beats wildly.

Mas steps next to me. "Ark, get on with it, then step outside."

Ark watches me as he reaches for a sack tied to his kilt and drops it on top of the pile of other gifts.

"Take a look, female," he says. "You will be most pleased."

"What is it?"

"You'll have to open it and see."

Mas bends to whisper in my ear. "You touch it, and you accept it."

"Thank you," I say. "I'm honored."

In approval, Mas nods.

But not Ark. He won't give in. He picks up the sack and pulls out a lavish blue silk dress, the kind worn in the eighteen hundreds on Earth, with a large opening at the chest and shoulders. It's beautiful, completely out of place around here, and I'm upset that he's staining it with his bloody hands. "Where did you find this?"

"On an alien ship."

I hitch a breath then shake my head. "We don't wear these

fashions anymore." It could be a costume for a play or the newest throwback fashion from Mars. They'd done the 2020s throwbacks last year and wore decorative masks.

Mas snaps his head up at the same time Ark turns. Several males start walking toward the door, crowding around it so I can't see what they're looking at. I rise on my toes, but that's no help, so I climb to stand on the throne and see over their heads.

Hart is walking up the bridge. Blood seeps from the many gashes covering his body. Even his kilt is torn, his ax is missing, and in his hand, he carries a piece of meat on the bone. I smile. My caveman. He fought a mighty beast of some sort and brought back food. It's mad and endearing, and I hop off the throne.

Mas steps in front of me. "Stay here."

I sigh. "Fine."

Mas walks to the window as the males part for Hart. As he approaches, I walk down the steps, hearing Mas shouting behind me. Reaching Hart, I look up into his unreadable eyes. On Earth, we underestimate the power of looking into each other's eyes. Another's gaze subconsciously tells us so much, and I didn't realize how much until I faced a male with no gaze. White eyes stare at me, and I don't know how to interpret them. I feel I should say something.

"Thank you," I say and put my hand on his, trying to get the bone. When he doesn't give it to me, I try to wrestle it from him because I'm starving, and he brought food. Saliva pools in my mouth at the prospect of finally eating.

Hart tilts his head and lets go of the bone. I take it along with the dagger from his kilt's weapon collection, then go to sit on the floor by the fire. "Thank you so much. I'm starving, and I was starting to think I'd have to eat the flowers just to keep from dying." I smile up at him and see more males gathering around the fire.

I hate to have to eat like an animal, but I can't be bothered with finesse in a place where guys walk around in kilts and compete for the right to spend a night with a female. I'm sure they won't find my manners upsetting. With that in mind, I slice off a piece of meat and, with the dagger, bring it over the fire, figuring the dagger will heat up, and it'll be like a barbecue. "If I had a wooden stick, I'd make a kebab. There's a lot of meat here. You want some?" I ask Hart.

All heads turn his way.

He seems bewildered, mouth slightly agape.

"You're hungry too, huh?" I continue. "Never had a kebab, I bet. At home, I'd put some spices on it and stuff, but whatever, I'm not picky."

Hart crouches, and his other pair of eyes lurks behind the white. It's a little scary, so I avoid looking.

"You want a wooden stick?" he asks.

"Only if you have one. Thank you. I really appreciate the meal." My belly growls, and the males, as one, step away from me.

I look around and frown. Weird.

The meat on the dagger looks seared enough. I eat my steak medium rare, so I blow on it a few times and pick it up between my fingertips. Gonna ruin my manicure, but whatever. I pop the slice in my mouth and chew. A strong, tangy taste, but really good. There's no fat on the meat. It reminds me of filet mignon. Not chewy at all. Practically melts in my mouth. "Mmmm," I moan. "Delicious." I nod at Hart, who puts a hand over his mouth.

The others do the same.

I cut another slice and bring to the fire. "What?"

"Nothing," a male says and makes his way through the guys. Hart's brother.

"Hi again," I say.

"I found a stick." He hands me a paintbrush.

"Perfect. Thank you." I slice four cubes of meat and stick them on the brush, then stand so I can hold it with the brush away from the fire and still cook the meat.

The males stand back again, their eyes wide, hands over their mouths.

"Why are y'all being weird?" I ask. "Do you not barbecue anything? Is it the stick?"

Hart walks up, eyes a blaze of orange. "We don't consume our own flesh or the flesh of another predator."

What's he saying? Wait, what? Ooooo! I throw the kebab into the fire. Bile rises in my throat, my belly along with it, and the chewed-up meat is stuck in my throat. I wanna swallow it so I don't vomit, but I can't. I put a hand over my mouth and close my eyes. Gross. Gross. Gross!

"Is our flesh not appealing to you anymore?" Hart asks.

I snap my eyes open and shake my head.

"Why not?" I can't read his emotions from his eyes, but I sure as hell can read the pinch of his lips. He doesn't appear or sound happy. If I say it's appealing, it means I wanna eat them all up, and they might kill me. So that's an automatic no. If I say it's not appealing, I might offend them. I'd rather offend. "Not anymore."

"A moment ago, it was delicious."

"I didn't know it was a *who*, you know. Why would you bring me this?"

He doesn't answer, but his shoulder bulges, bone trying to push forward. Oh no. Hell no.

"Hart, listen. We have a…a giant misunderstanding. I'm sorry I ate a piece of your male. Can we forget about the whole thing?"

The males are looking between their Kai and me.

"Unlikely." Hart walks back to the throne and sits, a stern expression on his face. "Leave us," he says firmly to his males.

Some of them shuffle toward the exit, others linger, still

staring at me. Slowly, I walk toward the throne and stand on the disk I know drops into Hart's chambers. I hope he makes us disappear from here. Suddenly, his chambers are the safest place to be in this world.

I ate one of their people. This means I'm a designated predator, and I know what happens to predators among a throng of other predators. They get slain.

CHAPTER ELEVEN

HART

When I brought back a piece of Sor's flesh on the bone, never in million moons did it cross my mind that my gentle flower-loving alien would eat it. Never. I am shocked to my very core and unsure how to approach her dietary requirements. Which was why I asked my males to leave us alone.

In addition, I need some time to think and come up with something for tomorrow's games. Are they still going to compete? I don't know. Who wants a male-eater in their bed? Only me, hopefully.

I extend a hand and groan, for Sor managed to tear out a chunk of my muscle right above the hip, the tender, flexible muscle where the hunting-form transition begins. The female takes my hand, and I notice hers is clammy. Inhaling, I smell her fear.

Ark is lingering by the door.

"You want to die?" I ask. "Because if you try to harm her, I'm gonna kill you."

"You're too weak now."

I *am* too weak to fight him now. "I'll let my alien female consume you, then."

He laughs. "Unexpected turn of events."

"I'll say."

"What now?"

"Now you quit the games, Ark."

"Fuck no. A predator on my cock sounds great to me."

"Until she bites it off," my alien says.

Woooo.

Ark's eyebrows rise.

I tug on Stephanie's hand, and she lands on my lap. "Ark, I suggest you get another predator. This one is taken."

"Two days of games left."

I sniff her hair. She still smells delicious, like something I wanna both fuck and eat. How can that be? I drop the throne into my chambers and close the opening at the top, but stay sitting on the throne. Stephanie turns in my lap, propping her bare feet on my thigh. My eyes follow the curve of her leg, my hand moving to squeeze her thigh. Smooth, leaf-thin skin. "I'd never have guessed you're a predator."

"I'm not, really. It's all a misunderstanding."

"I saw you eat one of my males with my own eyes."

"I thought it was beef or something."

I smile. "We don't eat what we don't know." I touch my nose. "We can smell food that's for consumption."

"Well, apparently, we can't."

Blood keeps trickling down my side. I'm getting light-headed, but I enjoy her sitting on my lap, so I linger a bit longer. I also enjoy talking with her. She fascinates me, and I want to learn more about her people. "On your planet, which species is at the top of the food chain?"

She scrunches up her nose. "The humans."

"See?"

"It's not like that for us."

"How is it like? Every planet has a species at the top of the food chain, deeming that species a predator and all others the prey. Otherwise, survival isn't possible. The food chain hierarchy is universal. All planets have them because every species has to eat. Energy doesn't create itself."

"That's true. Hmm." She's looking at the ceiling, so I lift my gaze too. There's nothing there.

After a while, when I'm still searching for what she's looking at, she says, "Let me put it to you this way. If you landed on Earth, people wouldn't eat you."

"What would they do?"

"First, they wouldn't let you land because we classify your kind as predators and you aren't allowed on the planet."

If not permitted to land on Earth, Ark, on his warbird, has likely hunted human ships carrying passengers, female passengers, to be exact.

"And second," she continues, pausing as I wipe my thumb over the inside of her thigh. "If you did end up landing, we'd be afraid you'd eat us."

Her arousal reaches my nose, and I wiggle it, pleased my touch arouses her. "How would you know to fear us?"

"All dual-forms predate on humans."

"Dual-forms?"

"Your animal form."

I bristle. "I am not an animal. I am a hunter. It is a natural part of me, not some sort of form."

"Oh, I'm sorry for offending you. We only have one form."

I accept the apology. She doesn't know better, and soon she will learn. "You've seen another *dual-form* on Earth? People like me?"

"No, but we study other species. We know."

Feeling more light-headed, I blink, my vision blurring. A whine at the back of my throat escapes.

"You're injured." She hops off my lap and extends a hand.

Frowning, I shake it, wondering why she needs to greet me again.

She chuckles. "No, silly, take my hand. I want to help you stand."

Groaning, I stand on my own, and the room swims. I stumble around the throne. The female tucks herself under my arm and guides me to the bed. I crawl over it and sigh, reaching for the medical panel to initiate a repair system when she starts yanking my verto. She wants to mate. Right now? Really? The sight of my blood must make her horny. She also wants to eat me and fuck me.

"I think you might be a goddess." I don't know which one, and I don't care.

"A goddess? Nah, I'm an IT tech. Can you prop up a little so I can remove the kilt?"

For once, I do as I'm told, and she strips me naked. Weapons clatter to the floor.

"Can you also turn the lights on? I can't see in the dark."

How can a predator not see in the dark? Strange, strange species. I pull up the panel and turn on the lights. The walls twinkle, and I dim them.

"Brighter, please." I do as she asks because I can't wait to experience whatever it is she has in mind. She's after something, but I don't understand what.

"Oh my God." She puts both hands over her mouth, her gaze glued to my side, near my hip bone, where a piece of flesh is missing. I look too. "What?" I ask. "It's nothing. I survived and won the first night." Blood's soaking the bed. I'm losing consciousness. I need to get the repair system going. Why is the alien fascinated with my wound? It will heal.

She looks around the room and throws up her hands. "Where the fuck is gauze or towels or a fucking hospital?"

She's becoming hostile. "Easy now, killer."

"But you're missing a chunk of your body."

"I know, which is why I need to initiate the repair system." I squint at the panel glaring at my face.

"What are you waiting for?"

"For you to back away from the bed. I can't believe I'm saying this, but I can't mate you in my current condition."

"What?"

"Mate."

"I don't want to have sex, Hart."

"Then step away from the bed."

Stephanie moves back, and I lock my jaw so I don't scream or grind my teeth. Here goes. I hit the panel and initiate the repair. It starts from the top of my head, absorbing the blood in my hair and fixing even the tiny broken ends of my hair, moving down my face, searing into cuts on there, over my neck, down my front. My muscles start twitching, bones rearranging, my hunter ready to come forth, but I can't leave this *form* now. It could knock me out, and my female would mate me if I weren't injured.

I close my eyes and imagine how I'm gonna mount her, how my hook will detach from my dick and latch on to her womb, and still I can't escape the searing pain. The repair laser lingers around my hip, and it feels like thousands of needles are jabbing my wound. It's duplicating my flesh to make new flesh.

Stephanie watches me, her expression one of horror. "What is happening to you?"

"Repairs," I say from between clenched teeth.

She steps forward.

I put my hand up. "Stay back."

The skin repair is the most painful. My claws dig into the bed as the repair system starts dragging my skin over the wound, then duplicating it, stretching, relaxing, making new skin to close the wound. Blackness seeps into my vision, I concentrate on her face, see if her image can keep me conscious. Mounting her. Breeding. Keeping. Taming this predator would be my life's purpose.

The repair system blinks.

I breathe out, then in because the hip repairs are coming and that's the biggest wound, meaning a longer repair time, and more pain. I brace for the worst, and it comes. The repair system sears to the bone. Not realizing Sor damaged my bone, I scream in pain and become a hunter.

I'm angry at the pain.

My vision is red.

I lift my nose and extend my flank, allowing the repair system to work. Lying down, I keep sniffing, swallowing the whimpers of a wounded animal. I wanna lick my wound, but if I healed that way, it would take too long, and I don't have time. I must hunt tomorrow and on the final day of the games.

From outside the repair system, Stephanie's fear penetrates my brain. But that's not all. The lingering scent of her arousal drives me mad. *Mine mine mine.* Skin stretches over my hip, and I roar, digging my claws into the bed, shredding the mattress. Feathers burst from it, and I keep clawing, biting at the feathers flying around me, mad I can't mark her. I want to mark her now, not after the games.

The repair system beeps, signaling its retreat.

Once clear of all lasers, I hop off the bed.

Stephanie steps back.

I peruse her.

She keeps moving back, and I corner her against the wall. I sniff her leg, up her thigh, tuck my nose under the fur covering her, and lick my teeth because the smell here calls to me. I take the fur between my teeth and tug.

Stephanie shakes her head. "Bad Hart," she says.

I tug the fur again.

"No." She tugs back.

I think she likes my other *form* better. I reshuffle my bones to stand as a male on two feet. Her eyes drop to my shaft, and I step back so she can observe my fitness, ensure all injuries have been thoroughly healed, and I'm fit to mate.

Stephanie moves around my body. She touches the back of my thigh and runs a hand down my leg, and my dick starts leaking semen. I enjoy the feeling of her hand on my skin.

"Wow, it's completely healed."

I grab her wrist and turn slightly, moving her palm over my thigh and up over my ass, to the front over my hip, and I close her palm over my shaft. There, I let go of her hand, and she moves it up and down, then grabs me with two hands. She strokes, spreading my fluid all over my dick. I swipe some of my seed and mark my lips, then hers, telling her in the language of my lands, I'm gonna mark her as mine, promising her I will win the games *and* her affection, something much harder to win than the games.

She licks my seed and swallows.

"That's a good pup," I tell her. "You want more?" I'm not asking, really. I press my lips against hers and kiss her, depositing my seed on her mouth so she can lick it off. And she does. "What a good pup you are." I unlace her fur in the front and part it to feel her breasts, the same places my pups will suckle in the near future.

I squeeze her nipple, and Stephanie whimpers. I keep my mouth brushing hers as she pumps between my legs, and then I twist her nipples, scenting her arousal blossoming in the room.

"Yes, pup, keep pumping. How much seed do you want, hm?"

Stephanie drops to her knees, her small, clawless fingers splayed over my thighs. Her wide tongue feels smooth over my length, and she licks from the base to the top, lingering on my hook, circling it, then lapping up the seed seeping out of the opening. Her eyes roll into the back of her head, and she wraps her lips around my top, then starts moving her mouth over my dick, effectively making me fuck her mouth. I'd never experienced anything like this or even thought about it, but I catch on quickly.

I press her against the wall more so that her head rests against it, then spread my legs wider and pump into her mouth. "You're a greedy pup. You want all the seed."

While she holds my thighs, tearstained big brown eyes stare up at me. I fuck her mouth, enjoying how it feels when my hook hits the back of her throat. It stimulates seed production even more, and my balls tighten, drawing up. As if she knows, she grabs them and gives them a squeeze. My body locks, and I stop moving. Ohhhhh yes. My seed rushes into my shaft's channel, spurts out, and fills her mouth. She gulps, and I hold her throat, making sure she swallows every last drop. She does.

I crouch at her eye level and lick my seed off the corner of her mouth. "You ate all my seed."

Red colors her cheeks.

"This is all very...alien to me. But I like it. I'm keeping you. You're mine. The games? Charade to keep my males occupied. When I win, and I *will* win, I will mark you, female, and you will give me pups. Do you understand?"

I lean back so I can look into her expressive eyes.

"Yes, Alpha," she says.

I kiss her mouth. "That's a good girl. Tomorrow, I'll bring you more flesh."

"Oh, that's not necessary."

"It is. Day two is provide-for-the-female day. We hunt for whichever food you like best. I'll bring you a treat. You want Ark?"

"Oh noooo. Is there chicken?"

I don't know what that is. "No chicken."

"Beef?"

"No."

"A rabbit even."

"Ark?"

She takes my face between her palms and kisses my nose. "Ark brought a dress. Makes me think there's another woman somewhere. Is there?"

"If there is I'll find her."

Stephanie nods. "I'm tired, Hart. Are you tired?"

Yes. "No, I'm never tired."

She smiles. I think she knows I'm lying.

I peck her nose too. It seems like something females of her species like after they swallow seed. *All* the seed. In the back of my mind, I'm plotting how I'm gonna secure more of these females for my males, even knowing they'll kill each other competing for this one.

CHAPTER TWELVE

STEPHANIE

In the morning, we're back in the hall, and Hart lounges on the throne, stroking my thigh in the same way I'd pet a kitten on my lap. Except, I don't purr. He purrs, quietly, like a sated big cat hanging from a branch, enjoying the sun. I think he's faking the resting state. I think he's taking the temperature in the room, from the males who're glancing our way. Though I notice none of them meet his eyes, only mine, I try not to acknowledge them and their painted faces and bodies. I try not to show fear when their bones visibly move under the skin, when the muscles flex, bulging in unnatural-to-me ways.

Hart leans in and brushes his cheek with mine. His beard rubs my skin as he whispers at my ear, "Your diet puts me in a difficult position."

"It's really not my diet, Hart. I also eat potatoes."

"Today's task is to provide. It means we have to provide the finest food, not only to prove we're great hunters, but to show our skill and catch a difficult-to-catch prey."

"There. You said prey, so it's not one of your males."

"Ark isn't one of mine."

I turn in his lap and see he's staring forward, so I turn back to Ark, who stands at the bottom of the steps. He dips two fingers into some ink and paints a line across his throat. Under me, Hart's body tenses.

"What's that mean?" I ask.

"He knows I'm coming after him."

"And?"

"His tribe and my tribe have warred ever since we walked this land. There have been brief periods of peace here and there only to rest the males. A truce has never been signed in blood until he and I signed it."

"If you go after him, you'll break the truce?" I ask.

"Yes."

"Don't go after him."

"I need to feed you, and you said our flesh tasted delicious. If not Ark, the alternative is one of my males, and I can't do that."

I purse my lips. "If he knows you're coming after him, why is he still here?"

"Because he's a lunatic."

My belly growls loudly, and I pat it.

In the cathedral, silence falls.

Oh God.

I stare at the floor.

Hart lifts my chin with his claw. "Shall we start the games, then?"

"No, Hart, I don't think you should. And if you do, because I'm sure you will, I'll have you know I love chicken more than…"

"Sor?"

"Yes, Sor. I love fried chicken, grilled chicken, teriyaki chicken." He's staring at me because he's never heard of chicken or beef or rabbit or anything. "Mashed potatoes?"

Hart shakes his head.

"Any other animal will do," I say.

Hart stands and takes me with him, then puts me on my feet and walks to Ark. He dips two fingers into Ark's cupped hands. Ink drips from his fingertips as he swipes his lips again.

"Where is your Sha-male?" Ark asks.

Mas climbs the throne steps, looking even more annoyed than he did yesterday. He doesn't spare me a glance, even though he walks right by me.

"Good morning to you too," I huff before I sit on the throne, violently hungry. My belly cramps. I haven't seen a single plate, fork, kitchen, or anything since I landed. They hunt for food. They have no need for cookware of any sort. "Whatever or whomever you bring, I won't eat it. Just so you all know."

Hart marches back up the steps. "You will, female."

"I will not."

His lips press together, and I grab the back of his neck, trying to bring him down so I can whisper in his ear, tell him it doesn't matter what he brings. I'd eat a bat if he brought it for me, but Hart steps back.

"The games continue," he announces. "But I forbid you from killing each other."

Murmurs start, then shouting, and I sort through the voices, trying to listen to what they're saying. They all want Ark. He's the only one in the games from another tribe, but Hart shouts back something about the truce and more females like me and bringing women here. "More females means more games," Hart announces. "This one is already mine. Everyone in the room knows this."

Protests erupt, and a roar rips from his chest. His muscles bulge. "This game is not once in a lifetime. I promise you. There will be more womankind. I will bring them."

"How?" his brother asks.

"I want to know too," Ark says.

Mas interrupts. "This female is here now, and that's all we have. Let's see… One hundred twenty-eight males left, so let the games begin."

Hart lifts his palm. "Out there, when you come after me, do not make me kill you. Any of you." He stares at Ark, then back at his tribal males. "When I come, lie on your back and exit the games. Tonight, when I return, I want the hall empty."

Ark laughs. "You can't order them what to do during the games."

"I just did."

* * *

An hour into the games, the cramps in my belly intensify. I'm so hungry that I could take a bite out of Mas's arm, the one that's flying over something I can't see.

"Mas, is there a… I don't know. I'm hungry and thirsty." I try to get up.

"You can't leave the throne platform, and you must watch the games."

I snort. "I can't see the games."

"They're on the screen in front of you."

"I can't see the screen."

Mas pauses, turns his head. "I don't understand."

"Me either, so that makes two people who don't understand, but that won't bring me any water, and I need water." And food.

"You would take water from me?" He waggles his eyebrows.

I sigh, propping my elbow on the throne and my head on my palm. During the games or maybe even after, I can't accept anything from anyone. "Forget it."

"About the games," he starts.

"Hart will win. I'll ask for water." Clearly, Hart is preoccupied with winning. Clearly, he doesn't know I need to drink and eat and use the bathroom. He understands nothing of me, and I nothing of him or the games or this new life I need to start living or else I'll die out here. A glance out the window shows my pod is still attached to the tower. "I want to go home," I whisper.

CHAPTER THIRTEEN

HART

On the Ra tribe side of the border, the portal Gur controls stands wide open. Only two males guard it, and neither is competing in our games. I creep up and knock them out, leap inside the portal, and see my brother midleap. Amti's pussy hole of all holes! Why is he tailing me? I scramble through the portal so it doesn't cut him in half and close it before my other competitors see us inside Gur's territory. I cross my arms over my chest. "Why are you here?"

"You're up to something."

He knows me well. I walk away from the portal. "Why are you even competing?"

He walks beside me. "There's nothing else to do."

I nod. That's true. Since we declared a truce with the Ra, we're finding ourselves rather bored and restless. Another reason the games are healthy for all of us, though not when they're fought to the death, and I need to remedy that. I want to take my brother with me, but I can't risk both of us for this. One of us should stay behind and inside our territory in case something goes wrong on this side.

To get rid of him, I need to give him something to do.

"You can't get rid of me," he says.

Mind reader, this one. I roll my eyes and keep walking, my boots sloshing through the mud. Bugs buzz around me, and I snatch one, put it in my mouth, and chew. Mmmm. I snatch another, eat it. I wonder if Stephanie would like them. They're like crackers, easier to consume with blunt teeth than most other prey. Does she indulge in crunchy snacks? I do. Sometimes, not always. I catch another one, but Nar slaps my wrist. I snatch my hand away and pop the snack in my mouth.

"Where are you going?" he asks.

"Go find Ark and bring the female his cheek. She'd like that. Soft red meat. You'll win the games."

"We both know neither of us can touch Ark."

"Well, I'm not killing any of my males either."

"You might have to."

I shake my head. "I'm gonna find another way."

"In one of Gur's villages?"

I stop, face him, and want to slap the smirk off his face. "How do you know that's where I'm going?"

"Mas told me."

Mas monitors the games and hears just about everything that goes on, so he clearly listened in on Ark's and my conversation. Mas is not allowed to interfere and compromise the integrity of the games, and he should've kept his mouth shut. Everyone deserves a fair chance at mating the female. Nar and Mas are close, sometimes I think closer than my brother and I. I'm a bit of a loner, while Nar enjoys the company of others.

"Mas talks too much," I say.

"Only to me."

"Then you know where I'm going which means you know you can't come with me. Go away."

He's marching with me, our boots slushing through the mud, scaring half the animal kingdom out here. We're not hunting, so there's no need for stealth.

"What are you going to do in the village?" he asks.

"I thought Mas told you."

"He only gave me the village name and said I should follow you."

Mas hasn't exactly compromised the integrity of games or what happens in the areas he monitors. If he overheard my conversation with Ark in the hole I dug yesterday, he didn't tell my brother about it, and I don't want to tell him either. My brother won't give up following me, so I might as well share what Ark and I talked about.

"Ark said Gur has a female," I tell him, "and he's planning to open the games for her. But it's a lure for us to enter. He'll kill the entrants, and if one of us wins, he doesn't plan to give her up."

There's no response, so I glance at Nar. He's got a... wishful expression on his face. News of another female will do that to males who haven't seen one in a decade.

"Ark had to bribe him to sign the treaty," I add.

Nar spits. "The Ra and their division will cost us everything."

"Ark wants peace."

"You can't trust him."

"In this I can. He's not stupid. He sees no future if we war."

"And you're going to the village because...?"

Stephanie identified a womankind dress Ark brought to her as a gift. "To confirm Ark's story."

"I thought you trusted him?"

"About peace, yes. About the female or Gur's plan? Not entirely. I need to see the female that looks like my female."

"She's not your female, brother. Why don't you understand that?"

My muscles bulge, and my bones move around. I snarl. "She is mine."

Nar shakes his head.

We're almost out of the Jamud area and into the clearing before a hill where Ra males patrol the border. I stop and assess the clearing, then the hill. Two males lounge in the grass, both in hunting forms, both dozing, bathing in the midspan sun.

"They're not sleeping," I say and tsk. Too bad. "We'll go around, come from the east."

"That'll take all afternoon. Then we have to cross the river, find the female, and get back same way."

I change into hunter and bolt east. My brother is right. I'm risking day two of the games. If I don't make it back, I'll lose this day, allowing a male to spend a night with Stephanie. But Stephanie won't accept a gift from another male. As I run through the mud, cutting across a difficult-to-cross quick-mud area, I think that perhaps, just perhaps, the goddesses haven't abandoned my people. They blessed me with a loyal female who has no reason to be loyal or trusting of me. Maybe she really is a goddess in the flesh.

* * *

Wet, tired, and annoyed that both Nar and I slipped on rocks and cut our flanks, we hide behind a weapons storage shed and lick our wounds before we attempt a stroll down the village street. We stink of blood, and other males will smell it, pay attention to it. Nar finishes first and sneaks inside the storage room. I'm almost healed when he walks out dressed in one of Gur's subtribe male uniforms and hands me the same sort of outfit. I also dress, and we stare at each other.

The Ra wear iertos. Heavier than vertos to begin with, they are also adorned with belts and jewelry that weighs them down in battle, and I'll never understand why they keep these old fashions when they know it makes them less agile.

Nar and I swipe mud off our boots and cover our tribal tattoos, identifiers of the Ka tribe on our faces. We spread the mud on our clothes and hands to look like we were working on something.

Rounding the storage shed, we step onto the main road, our boots sinking into the ground. It's muddy out here. It's always muddy due to heavier rains than what we get over in Kalia, our main town. We keep our heads down so as not to be recognized, but scan the huts we pass as we move down the path. Many males are sitting on stools, sharpening their weapons. A training drill is in full swing up front.

I glance at Nar, who returns the glance and nods, telling me he sees what I'm seeing. Gur is preparing an army. There's gotta be two hundred males whose attire I don't recognize at the border, and the tents at the edges of the village mean those males came to him from elsewhere. From where? Fucking Ark failed to mention this.

At the end of the village, we enter a newly set-up warrior camp and wade through the tents, again falling into line with warriors, disguised as one of them. It's clear these males are mostly strangers to one another, which is a good thing, but that also confirms that another subtribe has joined Gur's efforts. How many more want to invade my land again? How many will try to take Ark down and replace him? He's in trouble, and that's likely why he'll need a stronger alliance with me.

Well, I won't be solving his people's problems. I want to be sure he can deliver females like he said he could, and also that Gur has one for the games.

But I can't fucking see her anywhere.

We make it to the end of the camp and stop there.

"No female," Nar whispers. "Found an army instead."

I nod. "We head back. Double-check."

Turning, we move against the flow of males, bumping shoulders with many of them walking the other way. I wanna snarl and start ripping into them. Their scent of dominance and violence offends my Alpha instinct, and I wanna crawl out of my skin and fight them all, taste their blood on my tongue, hear their flesh tear.

Nar bumps into me, pushing me to the side, away from the walkway. We huddle near an unoccupied tent. "What the fuck are you doing?" he hisses at my ear. "I can smell you. Makes me itchy."

"I know, I know." I flex my claws, look around, trying to shake off my hunter when I scent something familiar. A human female. I bend lower and sniff the tent's flap. Faint, but I swear by the goddess, it's the scent of a womankind. I part the flap, and step inside. My brother follows.

"Same transport system as the female we got," he says about the white pod before us.

"You mean my female?"

Nar grunts, bumps my elbow. He picks something up, then holds it out. It's a shoe unlike any other, but an alien shoe nonetheless. I snatch it from him, examine it. There's no cover on it, just the bottom with something to attach the rest of the foot on the top. It's small. Female. Has a flower. I pocket the item.

The pod door is slid wide open, and in front of it is the other pair of the same shoe. The drag marks on the ground tell me Gur's males dragged the female out and she lost her shoes. I pick up the shoe and pocket it as well.

Two bags sit inside on the pod's floor. One small and pink. One is bigger and blue, and out of the top, clothes stick out, telling me Gur's males rummaged through her belongings. Entering the pod, I pick up the two bags and consider leaving, but there's no way I can walk out with these items unnoticed. "Get in," I say.

Nar tilts his head. "Why?"

"We're stealing the pod."

"How?"

"By flying it."

"You know how to fly this thing?"

"Mas does."

"Mas isn't here. Are you all right?" He knocks on my head.

I bat his arm away. "You said Mas has probes out searching for the pods."

"So?"

"So if I fire this thing up, he'll pick up the pod's signal."

"You hope."

"Yeah."

Nar squeezes inside the pod with me, and closes the door. When we can't fit in comfortably, I sit on the chair and move him to sit on my lap. Neither of us speaks for a beat, and then he turns all hunched down because the roof is so low. "We tell nobody about this," he says.

"It's most awkward," I say. "Don't wiggle. I might get hard."

"I hate you."

I want to laugh, but I snort instead, then move to the side, trying to see the panel past Nar's massive body. The panel is nothing like the portals or Ra warbird controls. There're only three things to do, and they come in three colors. Green, red, blue.

"What now, genius?" Nar says.

"Pick a color."

He points. "The red one here."

"What's it do?" I ask.

"Let's find out." He presses the button, and the pod lights

up, blinks a few times, and shows me a long white line with a smaller red line that's flashing, though I have no idea why or what it is, but the pod is on and Mas should pick up the signal.

Outside, we hear males speaking. They approach the pod and bang on it and keep banging before one calls for Gur.

"We should've stolen the female." From the backpack on the floor, Nar lifts a tiny piece of clothing shaped like a triangle to his nose. His eyes widen, and he licks it, tasting, humming a little. He licks again, partly salivating all over the small cloth. "Delicious female."

It looks like the piece Stephanie would wear to cover her pussy. I slap his wrist. "No, and you're not competing in Gur's games."

"Maybe I'll steal her."

"Nar, if you steal her, it'll start a war."

"She smells nice."

"I think they all smell nice, Nar. I think they're made of lust and madness."

"Amti," he says and shakes out his shoulders. A shiver visibly runs down his spine.

"Amti," I repeat, remembering how I called on her and then pissed on the fire, effectively marking the goddess.

The pod lifts, ripping through the tent's roof. Inside, we cheer. Outside, weapons clash against the pod's sides. Someone throws an ax and cracks the door.

"Hurry up, Mas," I say to the pod.

CHAPTER FOURTEEN

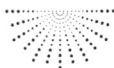

STEPHANIE

Most of the males come back wounded. They bring either their own flesh or the flesh of their tribal members and lay it at my feet. The scene makes me even more nauseated and fatigued.

They limp, some moaning quietly as they go about bringing in wood, building the fire like they did last night. The smoke starts filling the hall and makes me light-headed, even tired. I hold my head with a hand, wishing I could drop the throne on my own and go lie down on the shredded feather mattress downstairs that smells more like Hart, all woodsy and heavy with a male scent I can't quite associate with anything on Earth.

I glance at the tower and see two pods.

Blinking, I try to clear my vision. I'm seeing double. Great. Just great. A dull headache drums at the front of my forehead, and I feel like if I don't eat or drink something soon, it'll spread over one side of my face, giving me a migraine right before I pass out.

Where is Hart? He's late again. The sun's disappearing,

and I'm beat, even though I've done nothing all day but sit in the chair and watch Mas move around, which in itself gives me vertigo. I check on him over by the fire. He's not there, but I spy him walking along the walls as if reading them.

Mas seems restless, more than usual. He's pacing the entire hall, mumbling to himself, pausing to look at me, then snarling. Fatigue makes me not give a shit about his theatrics. Even more so because there's flesh and blood everywhere and these males shouldn't have done what they did. They're desperate to secure a female, and I feel bad. If I could call someone on Earth, I'd tell them to come. There're women who would be happy to do what I did and shack up with these dual-form aliens. Predators aren't what we portray them to be. Not for the most part, at least. And definitely not to me.

Hart walks into the hall, and I sit up, trying to keep my head above my shoulders, but finding it hard. He's wearing a one-piece dark-green kilt, with several belts over his torso and heavy armor over his wrists and biceps. As he moves through the hall, he sheds the armor, throwing it on the floor. Belts fall next, and I smile, thinking it'll be just like him to strip off the kilt in front of everyone and let me admire his fitness.

Hart reaches the throne and hands me a blue backpack and a pink purse.

Well, that wakes me up. "What's this?"

"Don't know."

He kneels, and I feel him doing something to my foot. It tickles, and I try to snatch my foot away. When I can't because he's holding my ankle, I move the backpack to the side so I can bend and see...a blue flip-flop. I wiggle my toes, noting it's a size too big. Still, a nice gesture.

I dig into the backpack and feel him slipping on the other flip-flop. Inside the pack are clothes, makeup, and hair care products. In the purse, I find a phone. It's out of battery. Gum. Lip gloss. Two strips of prescription meds taken once a day, so sixty days' worth of pills. I don't know what they're for, but the person these items belong to might need them.

"Where did you get this?" I ask.

"Found it."

"I know, but where?"

"Around. Do you like it? Accept it?"

I'd hoped he'd bring food and water, but I'll accept whatever he brought. It's just that now I'm aware there's another person, likely a woman, out there somewhere, missing a blue dress, and maybe going through the same turmoil I am, and with none of the meds she might need. I can't ask Hart to return them because I have to welcome his gifts. Even though some males brought an animal, and even though they skewered that animal on a makeshift stick and are now barbecuing it right behind Hart. I'm so fucking hungry. And thirsty.

I lick my dry lips, then dig through the purse, remembering the lip gloss. I put it on. Oh, the gum. I unwrap a piece and pop it in my mouth, wanting to eat it, and so I do. I wanna eat the gloss too.

Standing, I smile, and the image of Hart starts doubling, tripling, before my eyes roll, and I'm falling. The last things I remember are Hart's eyes widening as he reaches for me.

* * *

Soft feathers. Hart's scent. His voice, his touch, and he's rocking me like a baby. I pry open my eyes and stare at the dim lights in front of me, then open my mouth to say something, but I'm so weak, I can't utter a word. The lights twinkle, and I watch them as I fall back to sleep.

I wake up several times during the night, but keep

drifting off again.

I crashed. Ironic, since I really did crash only a few days ago.

* * *

It's morning. I can tell it's morning because the sun keeps me warm. Hart's not here. I rub my eyes before opening them and turn to find out I'm wrong. Although it's morning, the sun isn't keeping me warm. It's fur and blankets and decorative plush pillows doing that job. Sitting up, I groan and bring a soft fluffy colorful blanket Hart must've covered me with closer to my chest. "Thank God."

A space opens inside the bedroom, and Hart walks in from outside. He's wearing a short dark-gray piece of cloth around his waist that falls above the middle of his thigh, exposing his strong, long, muscular legs. Those muscles flex as he comes around the bed and crouches beside it. His hair is down today, black, wild, and long, framing his face. I roll to my side and reach for a golden bead in his hair, rolling it between my fingertips. I touch his hard jaw, running a finger over his tattoos. "Do they mean anything?" I ask.

"They spell my name in Ka script."

"Get out. This is what your alphabet looks like?"

"Yes."

"In English, your name and the word 'heart' are similar."

He purses his lips and shakes his head. "No. My name means the one who rules them all."

"Top of the food chain."

Hart nods, then glances to the middle of the room and marches there. He extends his palms and takes something from someplace I still can't see and turns around. In his hands is a small black bowl. It looks like it had been cracked and repaired, glued together with melted gold. The gold repairs give it a unique look. It's beautiful and belongs in a museum on Earth. But that's not all that catches my eye. Steam rises out of the bowl, and the aroma of soup makes saliva pool in my mouth. Excited, I sit up as he returns to his previous position, crouching near the bed.

Shifting to face him, I cross my legs and stretch out my arms, eager to eat.

Hart pulls back the bowl and tugs the sheets away from my front, exposing my nudity. As his eyes roam over my breasts and belly and between my legs, his hunter-form eyes replace the white covering them. It makes my heart beat faster.

He hands me the bowl, and I practically snatch it out of his hands, then bring it to my lips. I sip. Fuck, yes. I groan as something like chicken soup warms my throat and belly. I gulp down the broth without chewing the finely chopped colorful veggies or meat—I have no idea what it is, really—inside it all too quickly, spilling some from the corner of my mouth. I search for a napkin. There isn't one, of course, so I wipe my mouth with my hand. "Is there more?"

Hart smiles, his eyes lighting up bright orange. "My sweet, sweet goddess. Never quite satisfied, always wants more flesh."

I chew my lip as I put the bowl on the nightstand. "Um, what was in the soup?"

"Does it matter if you liked it?"

"Yeah, yeah, it matters."

"Ark's little cock."

Bile rises, and I swallow. "Hart, you have to promise not to feed me anything besides vegetables."

"It was a joke."

"Oooo. Oh. You got me there." I laugh and rub my belly. "Tasty, whatever it was. Wait, was it anyone else?"

"Eggs and vegetables."

"Great. Great. I'll eat it every day for the rest of my days here."

The orange in his eyes flares. "Amti, you will eat it every day until the end of *our time*. I will not be one of your servants." He prowls over my body, forcing me to lie on my back. His lips touch my lips, and his eyes stay on mine. They're bright and fierce and hard to look at, but I do it anyway because these predator eyes, unlike the white ones, are expressive. I touch his arms, running my palms over his muscles. I like how hard he feels. He's carved out of stone and made for sex. I swear it.

Hart kisses me, lingering with his mouth at my lips, and whispers, "You're enjoying my fitness."

I run my calves over his legs. "Mmhm."

"If I penetrate you, I will be your only servant. Do you understand me?"

He wants to penetrate me. Who uses that word, penetrate? Nobody, but mankind should fall in line with what this alien is saying. "I don't quite understand, but the idea that you'd serve me is alluring."

He lies on top of me, and I let out a moan. His body feels warm and hard, and with his plush lips on my neck, I'm feeling frisky this morning. When he kisses me, moving his tongue inside my mouth, he also moves his body back and forth, teasing me with the large hard cock between his legs, making my inner walls contract. I want the penetration he promised.

I run my hands through his hair. Lush coarse black hair falls over his face, curtaining us. It's partially wet, so he's fresh out of the shower—lake— smelling like male and sex. So much sex. I lift my hips, nudging him.

A purr rises from his chest, vibrating over my breasts, and he lifts up the bottom half of his body to insert two fingers inside me. I moan into his mouth as he pumps me with his fingers, his kisses getting frantic. He's already fucking my mouth with his tongue. I fist his hair and try to bring him even closer, but unless I melt into him, this is as far as we can join.

Until he removes his fingers, parts the kilt, and penetrates me.

I gasp, and he rises on his arms, orange hunter eyes watching me. He purrs louder, like a tiger, and it's sexy and wrong. It feels forbidden, taboo, animalistic, but he's a male with all the man parts, and yet not quite. Slowly, he moves inside me, stretching me, and although I'm slick and wet, his girth and length are pushing inside, trying to create more room.

The purring intensifies.

Above me, Hart's upper lip curls, and his jaw expands to accommodate growing teeth. He's starting to move faster, purring louder and louder, and fucking me harder. I feel him in my belly. His length hits so high that everything feels full of cock.

The purr turns into a growl.

My insides twist, butterflies dancing in my belly. I'm excited, scared, aroused, totally consumed in how he's having sex with me. I reach to trace his jaw. He grabs my wrist, the other one too, and forces my hands above my head. My breasts jut out, and he lowers his body so my nipples rub on his chest as he moves above me. His jaw widens, revealing sharper, larger teeth. His pupils expand. His groin moves, rubbing my clit. Pressure develops in my lower belly. I shiver, but not from the cold.

He lifts his nose and sniffs, then snarls at me, pistoning faster.

I come with a scream and keep coming because he's pounding into me, seeking his own release. My muscles go limp and my legs part, letting him do whatever he wants in order to get off while I take a moment to watch him more closely. He throws his head back, exposing the cords of his neck.

"I just want to bite you," I gasp.

He yanks me up and sits on his heels. With a hand at the back of my head, he directs me toward his neck, forcing my mouth toward it. I lick his neck and taste his maleness, a spicy tang on my palate. He's so sexy. We're attached, and I feel him getting larger inside me.

"Bite," he growls. His voice is mangled, a guttural sound somewhere between human and animal that sends shivers down my spine.

I open my mouth and bite his neck.

Hart lets out a roar, startling me. A jet of cum gushes, and it's so forceful that I swear I feel it all the way to my womb. Because I'm holding him and I'm pressed against him, I feel his muscles shift, even hear the bones in his shoulders scraping together, and I look up to see him staring at me with white eyes. "You marked my hunter."

I smile, a little nervous about what he means. "I did?"

He kisses me. "You bit the most vulnerable part of my body. The neck. You bit and didn't draw blood."

"I have blunt teeth. Your neck is hard. I don't know if I can draw blood."

"Do you want to draw blood?" He sounds excited.

"No, I'm good."

He moves a stray hair away from my face. "Tell me, Amti, how many of these heat cycles do you need before you can conceive young?"

"Okay, um, I'm Stephanie, and I don't have heat cycles." I push against his chest, but he won't let up.

Instead, he frowns. "I scent a cycle."

"And I'm over you calling me another woman's name while you're still inside me."

"Amti is the goddess of lust and madness, the goddess I called upon and pissed on before you landed in the Hall of the Fallen. Our goddesses freely take up any form or shape and come to us to tempt us. Amti temps us into madness, which is what you did to me. I'm mad about you."

I have no words. I'm trying to process what he's telling me and need to buy time to formulate a reply that won't offend his beliefs, but I also need him to understand I'm no goddess. I'm Stephanie from San Diego, California, who tried to go on vacation and crash-landed on his planet.

I hug him and, through the window, find the white speck on the tall tower. My pod, except now there are two pods, indicating there's another human woman somewhere around here.

Sooner or later, someone's gonna figure out where these pods ended up and come looking. When that happens, the human race will discover this race of predators.

"Hart?"

"Yes."

I lick my lips, swallow, think about what I'm gonna say next, but I have to say it because a part of me wants no harm to come to this male or his people, even if it means I'm signing off on never returning home. "You should destroy those pods."

He kisses my shoulder. "Why?"

"They'll track them, and they will come."

"Let them come."

"We are billions. We have warships and weapons of mass destruction. We can annihilate this entire planet in a matter of minutes." I haven't seen any modern weapons around here. It's all rustic and primitive, and the simplicity of it, the brutality of it all, makes my heart full. I kind of love it here. Secretly, I also kind of love this male. Nobody has taken care of me since the age of sixteen, when my mom moved to Mars. I've lived alone all my adult life. Not to mention, he treats me like I'm his personal goddess. I take his face between my palms. "Destroy them."

"I can't."

"Why not?"

"Because Mas needs them to look for the others. The pods emit signature signals, and he can find them and connect to them, then maneuver the lost ones to us. It could mean more females. And if the goddesses are pleased as Amti was pleased, they will bless us with many games and many young."

I shake my head. "But the risk it too high."

"Good thing I'm mad, then." He lays me down, then stands and stretches with his arms above his head. He's still hard, but the thing at the top of his penis is gone. He scrubs his face, glances toward the middle of the room, then at me, then back at the middle of the room. I'm sure there's some-thing there he's looking at, and I wanna ask about it and how I can fix my vision problem if possible, but his penis takes precedence, seeing as we just had sex.

"Can I ask you something?"

"You can ask me anything." He moves to put on the cloth and cover his bottom half, then pauses. "You're admiring my fitness again." He prowls across the bed, but this time doesn't lie on top of me. Instead, he flips me on my belly, lifts my hips so my ass is up, and practically climbs over me from behind.

He enters me, so big and heavy, his cock creates pressure in my lower belly. My eyes roll to the back of my head. "Oh my God," I choke out.

Hart fucks me from behind. "God is a fitting name for me, Amti."

Oh no. He pounds me faster, big heavy balls slapping my clit. "Oh yes, yes."

Madness and lust.

CHAPTER FIFTEEN

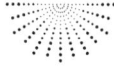

HART

Amti marked my hunter, and I released my hook. It attached to her womb, a marking of my own so that no other male can breed her. The hook carries my genes, and soon she will develop a new scent, one that repels other males and calls only to me.

Marking during the games is forbidden by the laws of the land and the secret scriptures themselves. Releasing the hook while mating is considered selfish, and the male who does it is shunned from the tribe like a traitor. Tribal females move from male to male and breed with whomever they please, usually with whichever male wins the games.

My father was shunned when he marked my mother. Once the males smelled his scent on her, they knew she could not be bred. Since my mother was a Ra princess, a highly fertile female of a strong bloodline said to be blessed by Bera herself, his actions led to another war, one more devastating than all the others, because the Ra slaughtered our females and our young.

But if Amti wishes it, I shall serve her in madness and in lust.

It's the middle of morning, and the empty hall tells me the males have gone out for the last day of the games. I didn't, which disqualifies me. I should be upset and displeased, but I'm content to lie in bed waiting for my goddess to return from the baths. She's climbed a few rocks and now stands under the waterfall, nude, enticing me to join her.

I stroke myself, running a thumb over the missing hook at the top of my dick. A male gets one hook for a lifetime, and he can mark one female, also for a lifetime. My dick feels weird without it, but the thought of her womb growing my young excites me. Blood rushes to my groin, and I stroke faster, watching her wash a place between her legs, thinking about how that tight place squeezed me. It's warm and moist, and I wanna penetrate her again.

The portal-control dashboard on the wall flashes. Someone wants to talk to me. Cock in hand, I don't open a visual, and I don't wave the control over to the middle of the room from where I normally work. I want to preserve this bit of time with her before I have to face my people and tell them what I've done.

The control panel detaches from the wall anyway. Mas is forcing an entry. I stop stroking myself and stand, grabbing the loose cloth and securing it over my middle. I walk to the control panel and shut it down. It flashes brightly, then dims, then dies out. Relieved, I sigh. I haven't closed a com center down here since…never. It feels wonderful not to be on duty.

Wrapped in a piece of soft cloth, Stephanie walks back into our chambers. She removes the fabric, and I smile, unsnap my kilt, and approach her. My goddess is insatiable. She steps back and uses the fabric to rub her hair.

I frown. I thought she wanted to mate again. "What are you doing?" I ask.

"Drying my hair."

We shake off water droplets, so I wasn't sure what the

rubbing was for. Hmm. Maybe she's content. Maybe I am the insatiable one, and any glimpse of her body tells me she wants me to mate her more.

Lust. I lust after her.

Stephanie proceeds to the sack I brought her yesterday, digs inside, pulls out a piece of blue cloth, and slides her arms through it. It covers her body, reaching just above her knee. A dress. She slips her feet into the strange shoes, if you can call them that.

"There's another woman out there, isn't there?" she asks.

"There is."

"Where?"

"In another tribe's village."

"But her pod is here." Stephanie points at the docking tower.

I nod.

"What's going to happen to her?"

I have a plan for her, but I say, "I don't know."

Stephanie sits on the bed, reminding me that I should replace the mattress I shredded during the body repairs. "We could go looking for her today."

I'm planning on that. "Will see."

The emergency portal lights up. I ignore it.

Stephanie eyes me, head tilted. She reminds me of a pup sometimes. Cute, small, harmless, curious.

I sit next to her to kiss her cheek. I linger, purring because I know that makes her aroused.

"When do the games start today?" she asks.

Here we go. "No."

A palm on my chest, she pushes, and I lean back. Squaring my jaw, I open the command portal and initiate a line with Mas, but only one way so he can hear inside my chambers but I can't hear him.

"What happened, Hart?" Stephanie asks.

"You happened. In my effort to win the games, I lost sight of what's important."

"What do you mean?"

"You have more fat reserves than I do, than most of my people do. At least twenty percent more, and I presumed that meant you could endure long periods of hunger. This is not the case. Half your body is made of fluid. Again, I presumed this meant you could withstand long periods of thirst. This is not the case either. I presumed a lot, asked little, and I was preoccupied with winning. When you collapsed, I realized I'd lost sight of you, my most important prize."

Stephanie's cheeks color, and she opens her mouth, then closes it, sighs, and fixes her hair. "Sometimes your bluntness leaves me speechless. I don't…" She shrugs. "I don't know what to say. Nobody has ever said stuff like that to me."

"I couldn't go out there this morning and leave you here unwell."

"What are you saying, Hart?"

"I lost the games."

Stephanie gasps, and the scent of her fear grates on my instincts. "Oh shit."

"That's not all."

Stephanie climbs up on the bed and sits with her legs folded and crossed. It would never occur to me to sit in such a way. By the time I untangled my legs, my opponent would have severed my head five times over. Strange, strange humans.

"Go on, Hart. What else?"

"After you marked my hunter, I released my hook inside you, effectively marking you as mine."

"Is the hook the thing at the top of your penis?"

"Yes."

"I wondered where it went. And, um, where inside me is it?"

"It's attached to your womb."

Stephanie scrubs her face. "What's it doing there?"

"Marking you as mine. No other male can breed you now."

"You lost the games because you'd rather take care of me than leave. Then, when you knew you were in the losing position, you marked me so whoever wins can't breed me. Is that right?"

"Yes."

"That…that disqualifies me as the prize, no?"

"Yes."

She smiles. "Why didn't you do it sooner?"

It's my turn to stare. "I didn't expect you to ask that."

She chuckles. "I think it's pretty obvious I wanted you to win from day one."

"Is it?" I grab her, bring her closer, and sniff her hair. Fuck, she even smells divine.

The emergency portal blinks a few times, signaling a forced entry. Mas really wants to talk to me. Groaning, I set Stephanie back down, regretting I didn't get a chance to tell her everything, including that marking is forbidden.

I open the portal to my males standing in the hall. They go quiet when they see me. Some, I notice, carry handmade crafts. Rur over there hand stitched a miniskirt over night. I had no idea my males could be crafty. It hits me then.

It's over. It's really over. I lost the games.

The Sha-male pushes through the males. Long gray hair drapes over the male's body covered with a black robe. He and I are often at odds, namely because I'd lost faith in the goddesses before Stephanie came, and now I have to ask him for a favor, one only he can help me with. Meanwhile, he came to the hall to declare and bless the winner.

When he realizes I have no intention of showing up in the

hall, he walks into my chambers, compensating for his lame left leg with a spear he uses as a staff. He believes the staff holds powers. I never believed it, but I also can't discount that the night before Stephanie's pod crashed on my land, I had called on Amti to come and pissed on the blessed fire Sha set up for the goddesses, effectively marking one for myself.

"Good morning." Stephanie stands and weaves her fingers through mine. "Or is it afternoon?"

The older male's eyes lock on our intertwined fingers, and he stops dead in his tracks. Turning up his nose, he sniffs, snorting at the back of his throat. Instead of greeting me or maybe slapping me like a parent would, he walks to my right, warily eyeing Stephanie. From the pocket of his robe, he pulls out some branches and throws them on the floor. He strikes them with the staff, igniting a small fire. Smoke rises instantly, and he mumbles a prayer, warding off evil spirits.

Usually, I'd put the fire out, but I indulge him and myself, because what if Stephanie really is a goddess in the flesh, or at least a blessing from the goddess Amti? I step back so the smoke doesn't hit me directly in the face.

"This is the Ka tribe Sha-male," I say. "Sha, this is…" I pause because I can't pronounce her name, and the only other name I can say for her is Amti. I don't say it.

"I don't know what Sha-male is," she says. "Is Sha his name or a title?"

"He's a male who has dedicated his life in service of the goddesses. He remains nameless."

"Oh, kind of like a priest. Hi, I'm Stephanie."

"Amti," the Sha-male says and lights up a feather, then leans the spear against the wall. "Amti, Amti, Amti."

Relieved, I sigh. "I believe so, yes."

"She has twenty digits," he says. "Ten on her hands and

ten on her feet. We only have sixteen. The goddesses have two seduction holes. Does she?"

"Yes." I need to make sure that the other pleasure hole gets penetrated too.

The Sha-male starts chanting, moving his hands back and forth in front of my face, then in front of Stephanie. He moves away, hitting the chamber walls with the staff, blessing them, calling upon Bera so she may give Amti young. Little does he know I marked the goddess already.

There's never a good time for this conversation, so I'll say what I have to say. "She marked my hunter," I begin and tilt my neck so he can see her teeth marks. He turns to glance and nods as if that's perfectly normal, which it might be. I don't fucking know.

"You have been chosen to serve the goddess," he says.

Going great so far. "Naturally, I returned the marking."

The Sha-male spins so quickly, you'd think he was a fledging on his first hunt. He's at me in seconds, and our chests collide. His hunter glares behind the white of his eyes. Not liking his aggression, I pull back my lip and growl a warning. "Stand back."

He doesn't. "How have you returned the marking?" He's shorter than I am, so he rises on his toes.

"I released my hook."

The Sha-male's jaw starts expanding, and his teeth sprout. He snarls at me and stabs his staff at the floor. "How dare you mark the goddess!" he roars.

At the sign of his hunter, I continue growling, my jaw flexing, readying to expand so I can lodge my teeth in his jugular and tear it out. I struggle with control, gripping Stephanie's hand tighter.

"Marking is forbidden. Marking a goddess is…is doom." He grips his staff, eyes now completely those of his hunter. But he struggles. He doesn't want to attack me. I'll kill him.

"According to whom?" Stephanie asks calmly.

We both snap our heads to her.

She swallows, and I smell her fear, but she continues, "Marking is forbidden according to whom and marking a Goddess is doom according to whom?"

The Sha-male doesn't look at her for long. He drops his gaze and steps back, tamping down some of his aggression. "According to our laws."

"Written by you, the mere servants?"

He glances up. "Yes, Amti."

"Your laws don't apply to me. I am the goddess, after all. And if I'm gonna be a goddess, let it be of madness and lust."

The Sha-male shakes his head. "No, no, let it not be madness and lust. Take whatever servant you want. A payment for all our mistreatment. I heard you were hungry and thirsty."

"I was."

The Sha-male glares at me. "How could you let her go hungry and thirsty, boy? Hm? Do you not fear madness?"

"Not really," I say. "Not as much as I fear that I'll have to kill my entire tribe when they try to execute a death sentence for the marking."

The Sha-male inhales smoke. "Your males haven't lost faith in the goddesses or in you, Hart. Only you have lost faith in both." The Sha-male walks away, but then turns. "There's another white pod on the tower. Perhaps you can secure another goddess. Perhaps this is the beginning of something better for us."

"Perhaps it is."

"Then do your duty and take your people with you."

I nod. "There's still a winner who has the right to claim the prize. Do we know who won?"

The portal opens, and Ark stands there, dressed in the Ra tribe's formal wear, the clothing he'd wear to his claiming ceremony. He smiles, and as the Sha-male exits, I close the portal.

"Shit," Stephanie says.

"You are clever. Do you believe you carry Amti in your flesh?"

"I'm not sure. We believe in one god."

"It's a male?"

"That's debatable, but I think so."

Strange. What would it be if not a male or a female? But I don't ask because she turns to me and continues, "I mean, what girl wouldn't want to believe she has a little goddess inside her?"

I nod. "Indeed."

CHAPTER SIXTEEN

STEPHANIE

Hart paces the room, thinking out loud, including me in the decision-making process. I don't think he understands how much I appreciate being included in the conversation that would effectively decide my fate on this planet. Because I *am* staying with him till the end of our time, as he'd said, and I want to know what's going on and how to behave once we do go up top and face his tribe.

The Ra and Ka tribes are neighbors, their hunters similar to each other in shape and form. There are other tribes on this planet too, but he doesn't mention where or how far or if they're a threat because he seems focused on the Ra and particularly the Ra tribal Alpha, Ark, the male who won the games when Hart didn't show up on day three.

Hart tells me of a female that landed inside Gur's territory. This Gur wants war. Ark and Hart don't, so they have that in common. Hart wants to come to an agreement with Ark, but he's not sure if Ark would want to fight him for me. While he's unafraid of Ark, he's also apprehensive about what Ark's death at Hart's claws would mean. The Ra tribe would seek revenge.

Winning in the games was one thing. Issuing a challenge to the winning male another. Not to mention, Hart marked me, goddess notwithstanding. This is a problem because, as it turns out, females breed and deliver young, then leave the young to be raised by the males so they can be bred by another male and so on and so forth. Females here have more freedom than males, it appears, and that makes sense seeing that their belief system is female-centric.

The markings on the walls and the art is all feminine, and yet, the males, from what Hart describes, are larger and stronger. It's a twisted power exchange that makes sense to him. Whichever male has a female or young and can also best all the other tribal members maintains power and is considered the top of the food chain and the leader of the tribe. Right now, Hart has what Ark needs to hold more power over his tribal members. If Ark secures a female and produces young, he's the Rai.

The Ra haven't announced their Rai yet, and even though Ark is presumed to be the Alpha of the tribe, until they announce the Rai, his status remains unofficial.

"Do you want to meet with him?" I ask Hart.

He grunts and walks over to the other end of the huge space that contains his chambers. With a swipe of his hand, he reveals another space, with plush fur for carpet and wooden stools arranged around a pit of some sort. I think it's a living room.

He sits on a stool and taps the one next to his. "Come," he says.

I join him.

A portal opens and reveals the hall once more. It's full of males, but only Ark steps inside our living room. He swipes a hand to close the portal and goes straight for me. My heart beats a mile a minute when he bends as if to whisper in my ear. Next to me, Hart's growl reverberates in my spine, and I lace my fingers with his while Ark pecks my cheek.

"For you," he whispers and drops a sack into my lap.

Hart snatches it, unlaces the ties that close the sack, and pulls out a red dress even more beautiful than the blue one. Claws extended, Hart rips it down the middle. Inwardly, I cringe. What can I say? It was a beautiful dress.

Hart's not done. He's slashing the dress with claws and tearing into it with teeth, fabric flying everywhere. Once done, he remains sitting, glaring at Ark as if nothing happened. I pick off a piece stuck in his hair. He snatches it from my hand and eats it. Okay, then. I think we've established that Hart is unhappy Ark brought a gift.

"Thank you, Ark," I say politely, not wanting to offend, mainly because I know Ark and Hart need to find common ground.

Ark takes a seat across from us. His gray-white hair is secured tightly behind his head, and he carries no weapons. "I won," he says flatly.

"I'm sure I'll be hearing it for the rest of my life," Hart replies.

"A short life if you decide to fight me."

"I doubt that very much, Ark. We've crossed paths before. We both know I'll tear you to pieces."

Ark laughs. "You're delusional."

Hart shakes his head, and Ark quiets, then wiggles his nose. "There's talk of goddesses walking among us."

"Just Amti," I say. "For now."

Ark's smirk drops instantly. He blinks and looks from me to Hart.

"Don't be scared," Hart says. "She only bites me." Hart tilts his head to show my teeth marks. I guess I bit him hard, because the subtle dent on his skin still shows. "I returned the marking, of course."

Ark knocks his knuckles on his head. "Of course." He snorts. "You selfish prick. If you'd showed up today for the games, we could've made a deal, and I'd have walked away. But now, you've placed us both in a fucked-up situation."

"I know," Hart says and leans his elbows on his knees.

"Why? Why? Why did you mark her?" Ark whines.

"The goddess made me do it."

I snort, holding back laughter. "He's mad, you see."

Hart nods. "Madness."

"That's my doing." I raise my hand.

Ark makes a fist and brings it to his mouth, eyeing me warily. I think the thought of sitting across from me freaks him out a little, but he won't admit it.

"You never competed for a female before, Ark. Don't pretend as if you give a fuck about her."

"I don't, but I can't simply walk away from the games I won. You need to give me something as a prize."

"I'll take care of Gur."

"Not enough anymore."

"Fine. What do you want?"

"Access to your portals."

Hart leaps up to tackle Ark, but Ark is fast too. He skips to the right, jumps, and appears behind me before I can blink. He yanks my hair and puts something sharp on the pulse of my throat. I think it's a claw.

Hart snarls, and his eyes lose the white and glow orange. "You hurt her and you're not leaving my chambers."

"Give me access to the portals so I can bring us more females. I will bring so many, we won't have enough cocks for them all. But I can't do this without you. Access to the portals and free passage for me and some of the males I take with me."

"Why do you need access to my portals for the females?"

Hart asks. Ark loosens his grip on my hair and pats my head, but won't remove the claw from my throat. Asshole.

"They chased our warbird," Ark says.

"They who?"

"The humans."

"And you shook them off before you entered our space, right?" Hart looks briefly at me, then back up. I hope the glance means he remembered what I told him about the pods.

"We shook them off," Ark says.

"How can you be sure?"

Ark remains quiet. He can't be sure.

"Are they a threat?" Hart asks.

"Yes."

"Where did you land, Ark?"

"Access to the portals, or I cut. She'll bleed like a baby lettig."

Hart's breathing hard, almost snorting, growing bigger, muscles expanding, eyes glowing. He's gonna lose it.

"Hart, please," I say. I have no doubt the male who holds me cares nothing for me, and he'll slice my jugular because beneath the male exterior lurks an animal, a predator, and a predator is ruthless when angered and let loose.

"Someone from the command tower will assist you," Hart finally says.

"That's not what I asked for."

"If I give you access to all my portals, you could turn around and show up in my chambers and kill us both while we sleep. No."

Oh my God. I swallow. Hart holds my gaze as if he wants me to do something. What? The goddess thing? Shit. "If you kill me, you'll never find your goddess," I stammer, while thinking of what else I could say that would scare Ark. "You will be cursed to walk the land alone while everyone else mates and their children grow. You won't die an honorable death, but die drunk on smoke from fire and lies." I touch his arm, and he jerks his hand back, then steps away, eyeing me warily. My heart jackhammers, and I'm scared shitless, but I square my shoulders because I think something I said bothers him and has made him release me.

"Come here," Hart says to me.

I hop over the stools to reach him and wrap my arms around his waist. He strokes my hair as he speaks with Ark. "If you think there's even a tiny chance the humans are able to track you here, you didn't take them to your home, and I know you didn't take them to mine. Where did you land the warbird?"

"On Mount Omila."

A shudder runs through Hart, and I look up as his jaw works.

"What's that mean?" I ask.

"You don't want to know."

But I do want to know. However, I don't interrupt the exchange. I know when to keep my mouth shut. They've barely calmed down, and Hart's producing this eerie low growl from his chest. God, this is some intense shit!

"Are the humans aware you…kidnapped their females?"

Ark snorts.

"Tell me!"

"Maybe. Maybe not."

"What do you think they'll do when they find out?"

"They won't find us. Not on Mount Omila. As you can see, I need the portals." Ark balances on his heels.

Hart scrubs his face and groans. "Yeah, I fucking see."

Ark shrugs. "Someone had to bring females. You should be thanking me."

"Get the fuck out."

"What's it gonna be, Hart?"

Hart plays with my hair, and I wonder if that somehow calms him. "I'll give you access to the portals of my choosing. For others, at the time you need them, you'll request access."

"Not good enough." Ark lifts a finger. "But, fortunately for you, I have somewhere else to be. This isn't over. We'll talk more later." Ark walks past us, and Hart turns after him. A portal opens, and it's not going to the hall. It leads to some sort of forested area, maybe the same place we visited when I picked flowers.

At the entrance, Ark turns. "Goddess of fire and lies, hm? I hope she's as sexy as you are."

"Motherfucker!" Hart lunges, but the portal closes, another one opening in its place, and Hart collides with the male standing in the entrance. It's his brother, who takes the brunt of Hart's impact and grunts.

"Heading somewhere?" Nar turns up his nose and sniffs. "Reeks of the Ra in here. Where's the body?"

"Nowhere. Sit down."

Nar nods toward me and sits where Hart sat, next to me. Hart starts pacing, telling him what happened between Ark and us just now. Nar's snarling as he replies while Hart's growling, and my translator isn't trained for the noises they produce, so I only understand bits and pieces. Hart thinks Ark's warbird was nearby when my ship was going down, and they saw my ship evacuating. Hart thinks the Ra warbird intercepted the pod's intended trajectory and sent other pods toward Ka territory, not Ra territory, so if anyone comes looking, they'll destroy the Ka first.

Hart's theory is that when the human warships closed in, Ark escaped, but to be safe, he landed on that mountain they mentioned.

"Ark thinks there's womankind," Hart concludes as he stops pacing and puts his hands on his hips. "Scattered all over the land."

Nar shakes his head. "Mas looked for crash sites."

Hart snorts. "I'm sure the Ra warbird blocked any signals, and even so, if the pod's down, the signal dies."

"We know of the one in Gur's village," Nar says. "Along with the army he's amassing."

"Yeah, feel like competing?"

Nar wags his eyebrows. "She tastes good."

"You've seen her?" I ask.

"Nah, I got something of her that tastes wicked." From his pocket he pulls out a G-string, puts it against his nose, and inhales loudly. "This is better than smoke. What is it?"

"Um, those are her panties. Underpants." Has he licked them to taste? Probably. I need to get used to their behavior. I really do. Maybe next year.

"I don't know what panties are or what's under them," he says.

"That piece of clothing covers the...the area between the legs," I explain.

"Why would you want to cover that?"

Hart lifts two fingers. "I think they're hiding the fact there are two holes."

I am mortified. "Can we talk about something else?"

"*Two* holes?" Nar's eyes are saucers.

Hart walks over and pats him on the back. "You wanna compete in Gur's games?"

Nar stands. "I'm on my way."

Hart grabs his wrist.

Nar snarls and shakes off Hart's hand.

"If you get squeezed out there," Hart says, "and you will get squeezed, the mission is to quietly kill Gur, not to win the female. Do you understand?"

Nar nods. "Yes, brother."

"Fuck."

Nar smiles.

"Wait wait wait," I say, and run across the chambers to grab the woman's medicine. I return and hand it to Nar, who tries to read the writing on the strips. "It's medication," I say.

"What for?" he asks, sniffing the packaging. He licks it. Yup, he definitely licked the woman's G-string.

"I don't know."

"How many does she need?"

"One per day."

"Span," Hart clarifies.

Nar portions off three strips, twists his lips, gets a fourth one. He hands me back the rest.

I don't take it. "She needs all her meds."

"Only one a span and one more for the way back."

I turn to Hart. "I don't like this."

"She needs to cooperate," he says in a tone that brooks no argument. "Take only four, Nar, and make sure she knows what you have. But remember, the mission is to—"

"Yeah, I'll kill him. Don't worry."

"Take Mas with you."

"No fucking way. You need him here."

"You need him more."

Nar rolls his eyes. "But he's so annoying during the games."

"I know. That's why he's going with you. Good luck." Hart claps him on the shoulder.

I expect Nar to stomp away on a mission, but he lingers.

There's a quiet, almost serene moment between the brothers where their eyes lock and they stand there, not quite willing to part. Awww. It's sweet how they purr in their chests and match each other's sounds. I'm about to step away, feeling like I'm intruding on a private movement, when Nar pulls out a dagger and slices Hart. I scream, terrified.

Nar swipes two fingers over the cut he made on Hart's

chest and brings his fingers to his lips. He licks the blood, purring loudly as if savoring the taste. "Thank you, brother."

"May Aoa be with you," Hart says.

Nar exits.

I feel as if a mountain of worry has fallen off my back. I think I aged ten years during these meetings. "Good Lord, Hart. I'm done for the day. Can we swim or anything besides talk to another of your males?"

He smiles. "They're your males too."

"Oh," I say.

"Not in the same way I am, of course." He raises an eyebrow.

"Of course," I reassure him. "I know what you meant."

"Good. You can do what you want. I can't. I have a hall full of males and lots of explaining to do. The portals are yours. I've programed the command center for your touch."

"Yeah, about that. I—"

Mas's voice intrudes from somewhere. "Hart, you can't send me away. I won't go."

"You are going," Hart says and winks at me as he leaves the room.

CHAPTER SEVENTEEN

STEPHANIE

Even when he rests, Hart's heart beats strong and fast. I bury my face in his chest and stretch out on top of him like a lazy kitten. His purr vibrates on my lips, and I look up, expecting him to be awake, but his eyes are closed, though I know he's not sleeping. Last night, he came home late in the night, a little edgy and a lot bossy, with the kind of pent-up aggression he likes to wear off by fucking me. We didn't get much sleep. Claw marks on the headboard and a soreness between my legs tell me we likely slept not more than a few hours.

I peck his plush lips. "I know you're awake."

He grunts, but won't open his eyes.

"Do you have to be in the tower today?" I ask.

"I'm sure they're expecting me."

"But?"

"But I'm not going."

"Oh, nice. Maybe we can stroll through town today."

He grunts. "For what purpose?"

"No purpose. Just walking."

"Aimlessly?"

"Mmhm."

He grunts.

I think that's a yes, and I crawl out of bed, put on the borrowed flip-flops, and stand. The chambers are full of glowing golden vertical lines. Some are stationary, some move around, some shrink into tiny lights, then stretch out again into a line from floor to ceiling. Multiple holographic-type screens blink and move around in the middle of the room. The control center.

I cover my mouth with a hand. "Oh my God."

"Yes?" he answers.

"I see them."

Hart vaults out of bed and appears before me in a split second. He crouches. "Who? Where? What?"

"The lines." I point. "I see the lines!"

Hart looks at me, and his eyes widen. He grabs my chin, lifts it, bends a little, looking right into my eyes. Behind the white covering his irises, I clearly see what he calls his hunter eyes.

He steps back. "What do you see?"

"Vertical lines everywhere. They're moving, flashing. And..." I point again, "that's the command center."

"Vertical lines," he repeats, frowning, then his pupils expand, and I see just how expressive his hunter eyes are.

Oh, this is wonderful. Finally, I see things the way he sees them. Of course he's confused. He can't imagine not seeing the lines. They're a part of his world, like air. "Portals," I say. "What do closed portals look like?"

He smiles. "I guess they look like lines." He scrubs his jaw. "Your eyes have changed."

It's my turn to look surprised. "What do you mean?"

"The color disappeared."

"That's freaky. Um, can you show me to the bath portal?"

"Do you need to waste or bathe?"

Eeeek. "I want to see my reflection in the water."

"Come." He moves toward two adjacent lines a few steps from the bed and gently touches the one on the right. A portal opens and leads into the landscape miles from here that we can access from our chambers.

He moves his hand from bottom to top and, like a zipper, closes the portal. "You try," he says.

My hand shakes as I stretch it out. Warmth hits me first, and I poke the bright golden line. It opens the portal. "Whooo! I can do this all day." I zip the portal with a swipe of my hand like he did. I open it again. Close it. Open. Close. Open. I glance at Hart, and he's giving me his best patient face. "Okay, okay, I'm done now." I step into the landscape and notice a tent to the left. Usually, there's nothing on the left. The path leads to the pond and the waterfall.

I walk inside the tent to see a rock that reaches up to my hip, with water flowing over it that disappears into a hole in the ground. I peek into the hole and can't see anything. It's pitch black. "What's this?"

"Private waste space," Hart says, lingering outside the tent's door.

I swallow hard, touched that he's figured out how uncomfortable I've been all this time. He knows too, because he winks at me. I walk to him and rise on my toes, but I can't reach him unless he bends his head. He does, and his pupils widen, flecks of gold dancing in the orange irises. I've never seen the gold in his eyes either. "Thank you."

"You must tell me of the necessities so that I can accommodate them. You must not suffer things that are easily fixed. Is that clear?"

"Yes, Hart."

"I'll bring the tree soon."

"Hm?"

"The tree for flowers."

I frown, not understanding.

"I've decided where I'll put it. Come see the reflection." He steps aside so I can walk to the pond and crouch beside it and see my reflection in the water. White eyes greet a familiar round face framed in brown curls. One curl slides off my shoulder and falls into the water. Hart crouches beside me, picks up the curl, and secures my hair at the back of my head.

"Why did my eyes change?"

When he doesn't answer I look up.

He stares ahead at the waterfall. "I don't know. I am… acquiring a healer, an old female to help you and other womankind, if any, with pregnancy and many other female things I can't possibly fathom."

"I thought there aren't any females left."

"She is too old to breed and not a Ka."

He will take care of me, and even though I can care for myself, it makes me feel safe to know I can lean into his strength.

Hart shifts from one foot to another, gaze still ahead, a gentle breeze moving his hair. "I love you, you know."

I stand and throw myself at his back, locking my hands around his neck and hanging on tight. Under me, his body shifts, and he becomes the hunter. Rearing back on his hind legs, he wiggles his ass, leaps, then splashes into the pond. Slam dunk just took on a new meaning around here.

From underneath the water, he detaches me and swims away. I kick to the surface and emerge to see him back on the shore, shaking off the water. He leans forward, and I swim to the edge, rising up on my arms, and touch my forehead to his hunter's forehead. Bright predator eyes stare back at me.

I kiss his nose. "I love you too, monster."

. . .

***

Hi, thank you for reading the first book in a new series. I am so very excited about these new guys. They're edgy, funny, sexy, and I wanna spend a year or maybe even more writing this Sci-fi Alien Predator Romance thing. Nar's story is book 2 with a teaser on the next page…

STOLEN - TEASER

NAR

Lightning cracks the sky, and the coming storm gathers the dark clouds as hundreds of predators assemble on the open field. The mud makes the already soft ground softer, and my boots sink lower. I lift a foot and move closer to Mas, leaning in. "How many are entering the games?" I whisper.

"Two hundred at most." He gives me a knowing look.

The prize is a womankind who crash landed in the Ra tribe territory, and both the Ra and my tribe, the Ka, haven't competed for a female in a decade, the games my brother recently held notwithstanding. After the wars between the Ka and Ra, my tribe was left with no females or young. Sterility plagues the Ra females, so they've got nothing too. There're over four hundred males in the camp and more in the nearby village, so why are only two hundred entering?

Mas and I know Earl Gur plans to break the truce that Ark, his tribal Alpha, signed with my brother, Hart, and that's why I'm here. To kill Gur in the games.

"Have you seen Gur?" I ask.

Mas shakes his head.

"Are any of our males here?"

"As far as I can see, only us."

A male bumps my shoulder, and I grunt from the impact. He walks on as if he didn't do it on purpose. Old wounds die hard, and the animosity between the two tribes goes back centuries. We've fought this tribe for either land or revenge, and sometimes for no reason at all.

"That's Feli, Gur's new second."

I killed the old second. "You think Gur's holding a grudge against me?" I ask. A rhetorical question. Every one of the Ras holds a grudge against the Ka, especially against me. I've slaughtered many of them on open fields like this one. That's why Mas and I stand alone and to the left of the wooden stage platform with a single chair that I presume the prize will sit upon as she awaits the games. "I wonder what she looks like," I say.

Mas side-eyes me, lifts a foot, and moves back a bit. I step back beside him. We're gonna sink in the mud to our knees if we wait any longer. A drop of rain hits my nose, and I turn up my face and squint. The sky's all but black.

"This should be fun," Mas says, face tilted up as well.

Competing on this muddy terrain while it's raining, and the clouds signaling a thunder storm as well? Yeah, should be fun. The two-hundred-and-some males shuffle. Whispers and hooting sound as Feli takes to the stage, his boots smearing mud all over it.

"Here we go," Mas says and cracks his neck. He gets off on being the finest portal master in the lands, and anyone who takes up portal controls during the games is his target, as portals are the way we travel across the land. Not to kill, though Mas has no issues with eliminating males, but more to wrestle portal control from the one who's running it.

Before pulling up the portal controls, which are a series of holographs that Feli will monitor during the games, Feli glances at Mas and smirks, swiping his hand over the control panel.

Screens pop up all around him, showing us the terrain Feli designed for the games. I recognize some local places here in the village, others in the middle of nowhere inside Ra territory, and one that looks familiar, as if it's one of our villages in the south.

"Is that what I think it is?" I ask Mas. If it is one of our villages, then Feli is telling us he has a portal hidden inside our territory.

"Possibly, but I can't be sure. I gotta get in there." Feli might have breached a territory inside Ka land, one that contains Mas's portal controls. While we all have entry points into each other's territories, we keep them secret so that our spies can safely move in and out of enemy land.

"Fuck. It could be a trap, Mas."

"I know, but I have to check it out anyway."

"You could get stuck in there for spans on end." If it's an illusion, a replica of our land to lure Mas and me into it, we'd get stuck inside a dead-end portal leading nowhere. Such illusions are hard to breach and could prove deadly if there's no way out.

"Don't worry about me. Worry about Gur."

"Yeah, well, he's not here, and separating us works to their advantage."

Mas presses a claw over his lips and taps them. "Where's the prize?"

I shrug as if I don't care while my fingers itch to reach into my pocket and pull out the prize's underpants, a piece of red cloth that hides the place between her legs. The scent has faded since I first found it, so I can't wait to sniff straight from the source. Just thinking about the smell makes me hard.

I adjust my erection.

Mas taps his nose, telling me he can smell I'm hard, and no amount of lying would convince him otherwise. Our Kai, the alpha of my tribe and my brother, sent me to kill Gur. If I can secure the prize, the womankind, in the process, that's great. But if I can't, Gur takes priority over the games. I should be worrying about where Gur is and not when I'll get to see the prize and how I'm gonna sniff between her legs.

"One hundred ninety-two males entered. Closing the games in…" Feli lifts a hand and counts. "Five, four, three…" I search for Gur.

"He's not entering," Mas says.

"Fuck." The games get deadly out there. It would be easy to eliminate Gur. Out here, killing a Ra earl could incite another conflict. If he won't enter, killing him with nobody seeing me do it becomes almost impossible.

Feli closes the entries to the games, and the bitchhole Ra cheer. Pissed, Mas and I growl low in our chests. We expected Gur to enter. An Earl usually enters even when he doesn't want the prize. It's a show of support for his people and makes for fantastic competition because everyone wants to beat up their superior for fun and games. Normally, you couldn't beat up an earl, or a Kai, in our case, or he'd kill you. That's why the games are fun. They always have been and always should be. But over the turns, our people and the Ra alike have grown so bloodthirsty that we don't know what fun means anymore.

Even my brother killed our own males during our games a few spans ago. It set a bad precedent, but I trust he did it because they left him no choice. I heard those males were protesting because he admitted a Ra tribal alpha into our games. It rubbed some of our males all wrong, and a sub-tribe formed, intent on killing my brother. During our last war, Ark, the Ra tribal Alpha, killed more of our males than I have of his, and that's saying something. Despite that, my brother let him compete and even let him win.

Rain pelts the weapons strapped around my waist, drops hitting the hilt of my dagger and ringing in my ears. I rest a hand on the hilt and wipe water off my face. It accumulates again, and I shake my head, annoyed I'm getting wet. Mas secures his hair at the back of his head and shakes off his body. We're predators, hunters, and we dislike standing in the rain.

The Ra males start growling.

Everyone's getting irritated because Gur's taking forever to bring out the prize. It's on purpose, I'm sure, to get us all worked up and agitated. If he's not competing, then he's watching the games and monitoring with Feli, sitting right near the prize, guarding her so nobody steals her. I snort. As if any male would stoop so low as to steal a prize instead of winning her fair and square.

Between the grunts and growls, I hear the males on the other side of the podium cheering, so something's coming. The crowd parts, revealing a moving green feather. Gur's easy to spot as he's always got this green decoration on top of his head. He thinks his mother was descended from Herea, goddess of the hunt, so he wears the bird's feathers.

Gur climbs the platform, wheezing a bit over his bulging gut. He's been eating well, slowing down. He couldn't compete even if he wanted to. Fitness is everything in the games, and the female will take notice of mine. Naturally. I'm fucking fit.

"Where's the girl?" I growl, then stare, needing no answer because Gur's climbing up the stage holding a leash attached to a female who's crawling behind him.

Silence falls over the camp. Even Mas adjusts his erection. A female on a leash teases our darkest fantasies, the ones I believe every male in the lands harbors since a very young age. We just haven't ever seen it play out in front of our eyes.

"Don't even think about competing for real," I hiss into Mas's ear.

He purses his lips, eyes twinkling with lust.

"I mean it."

"Quiet while I work out what I'm seeing. I can't believe he brought her out this way. It's so wrong."

"They're gonna want her bad."

"More reason for you to figure out how to kill Gur now and not compete at all."

"Yeah, let me just arrowhead him from here and walk away."

Mas chuckles.

We are so fucked. And not only because Gur is practically unkillable now. Ever since I found the underpants, I knew I wanted to sniff where the smell came from again. It's a breeding instinct, nothing more, nothing less. And I expected the same sort of female as my brother's female. But this one is smaller, thinner, with long black hair that's dragging in the mud left from Feli's boots over the platform. She's wearing blue pants like my brother's female, and a white shirt.

As she climbs the chair and sits with her head down, instinctively, I move toward her. Mas grabs my wrist. Turning toward Mas, I snarl when Feli shouts, "The prize!"

His shout breaks through some of the fantasy fog in my brain and brings me back to reality where we are two males against two hundred, not to mention the other two hundred are spread out between the camp and the village.

"We need to stay alive," Mas hisses, then releases my wrist. "Get it together."

I roll my shoulders and return to my place beside him. "Maybe she's ugly."

He snorts.

Yeah. If she's anything like my brother's mate—small, cute, submissive, with round, colored eyes and a perky nose —I'm fucked. Huddled in on herself, wet black hair shielding her face, she rubs her arms, looking lost and alone on a chair large enough to fit a grown hunter. Gur tucks a claw under her chin and forces her to lift her face. She slaps his hand away and leans as far as she can away from him. Which isn't very far.

He tries again, and she leans away more. At this rate, she'll fall off the chair. Gur grabs her by the throat and moves her hair away from her face, then steps back.

Pale face. Small nose. Pretty plush lips, colored blue-gray unlike red as I've seen on other humans. Slanted eyes with black irises in stark contracts to the white around them.

"Real ugly," Mas says.

"Mm-hm." I give him a side-eye, and sure enough, Mas is staring at her.

"You can't compete for real," I tell him.

"Neither can you," he reminds me. "Make it look good, but you're here for Gur's blood."

"I'm fine."

He glances at me and grunts.

The female turns her head, and we lock gazes. The world vanishes, and my heart beats loudly. I hear it in my ears. My hunter, as if waking up, takes notice of the female, stirring my bones, making my muscles relax.

Mas slaps the back of my head.

I wince and slap him back.

He points to his eyes. "Eyes off the prize, hooker." Hooker is a derogatory term for a male who releases a hook and marks a female. A selfish male who wants a female only for himself. Both my father and brother are hookers. I'm no hooker. Just because I find her attractive and pitiable on that platform doesn't mean I'm gonna compete in the games. And it definitely doesn't mean I'm gonna mark her…Read more!

ALPHA BREEDS TEASER

ALPHA HORDE BOOK 1

K ingsley

I get my phone and angle it for a selfie. The bright glare behind me is messing with my picture. I turn around in my chair and see something glowing on the floor. Oh, someone dropped their phone. Holding my cup carefully, I creep through the bushes to the fence, then set the cup down. This isn't a phone. It's a light coming out of thin air and expanding. "What the hell?" I slur. Someone must have slipped something into my drink. Fuck, I'm tripping. Better go back and sit in my chair.

I freeze and look around. I'm sitting on something soft. I look down and around, and it's a bed. A huge bed supported by a carved black headboard and footboard. It's a room, and it smells...sexy. My nipples perk. Holy crap, I'm turned on. Oh, shit, someone really slipped something into my drink. It's making my body buzz and making me see crazy things.

How did I get here? I was just gonna go back and sit in the lawn chair. Where's my beer?

There's a single nightstand, brown sacks on the floor, and some animal rugs. I have no clue what happened. I don't see a door either. Nothing but dark green walls made of no material I'd ever seen before. They're deep green, almost black, with gray scratches and cracks that look like wear and tear. I dare not speak in case a serial killer drugged me and stashed me somewhere in his den. Or maybe he's got an underground house where he's gonna skin me and make clothes out of my hide.

I try not to breathe as I scoot over the covers. I swear these things are made of skin too. It's not cotton under my fingertips, the bedding feeing more like leather. I get to the headboard and prop my hands on it, then lean over to see the floor. It's something like cobblestone. Dungeon. Someone stashed me in their dungeon of horrors.

Or I could still be sitting in the green lawn chair and tripping about the dungeon. Oh man, this is some seriously fucked-up shit.

A click sounds, and the wall in front of me slides open.

My heart stops.

My breath ceases.

There is a monster at the door. A seven-foot-tall sage-green creature with pitch-black eyes, no ears—no ears!—a short nose, protruding cheekbones, and a forehead that blends with his scalp because he's bald on top. We stare at each other for what feels like forever. At least he's blinking. I'm not doing anything. I'm frozen and yet hyperaware my body is buzzing with something. It's as if ants are running all over my skin and making my nipples hard.

The monster lifts his face. His nostrils flare, and he tilts his head as if confused. On the bed, I back up and hit the headboard. Nowhere to run. He's blocking the only exit. When he steps inside the room, all bets are off.

I scream at the top of my lungs and spin around. At the wall behind me, sharp objects I recognize as weapons are stacked on the shelves. I grab the first thing I can reach, a sword, maybe, and swing. It falls at my feet. Too heavy. I grab something smaller and throw it. The sharp circular thing spins toward the monster.

He turns emerald green. Some sort of…body plates form over his body. They're like reinforcement plates for his abundant muscles, and they cover every inch of him. The sharp weapon I threw bounces off. I scream like a banshee, reaching for everything on the wall, throwing things at him, but he stands there as if I'm not even trying. Then he peels back his lips and shows me four sharp four-inch-long canines, a pair of them on each side of his mouth.

He opens said mouth. The sound that comes out is unlike anything I've ever heard, aside from horror movies, of course. I scream back, now in tears. "Oh my God, save me. Oh my God, what is that? Oh my God, this is the worst trip of my life. I swear I'll never take drugs or drink again. Please, please, take me to the hospital. I can't take this."

I sit on the bed, pull my knees toward my chest, and cover my head. I rock back and forth for a bit, then look up. Oh Lord, the monster is still there. At least his body is back to sage green. The emerald body plates no longer cover his muscles.

"I'm tripping hard," I tell him. "And I'm terrified. Is Jill around?" Monsters don't exist. He could be a frat boy I don't remember meeting, and I'm the crazy bitch in his bed who sees a monster instead a California boy-next-door in surfer shorts and flip-flops.

The monster speaks.

It's a language unlike any other, mostly hissing and

growling. My throat and tongue can't produce these sounds, which leads me to believe I'm definitely on some hard-core drugs someone slipped into my beer. I gotta swim out of this and wake up.

The monster speaks again and moves away from the door. He motions with his hand. I think he wants me to leave. But I can't because I'm paralyzed on the bed, and I have no idea what's out there waiting for me. I'm afraid to get arrested. I'd lose my scholarship if that happened.

The monster stays quiet as he watches me. I hear a sound. It's barely audible. I think it's coming from him. It reminds me of the sound a rattlesnake makes when it shakes its tail. If he hisses at me, I will pee myself. "I don't understand you," I say and wipe my eyes.

He scratches his head, spins around, and I see his back. His hair starts in the middle of the back of his head. It's long and black, neatly braided down his spine. A pair of snakes are imprinted on his skin as glowing yellow tattoos. I'm making up some serious shit here.

The monster leaves, and the door slides closed behind him.

I'm alone in my own nightmare. My brain has conjured up monsters. The fear of losing my mind paralyzes me, and I grab the sheets and cover my body. I close my eyes and hope to God I sleep through this. Yes, I just have get through the trip until the drugs wear off. Then I'll find myself inside one of the frat boys' rooms, no worse for wear. Nobody's gonna hurt me. If the man who appeared in my mind as a monster wanted to hurt me, he would have. I'm just really messed up. That's all. Read more...

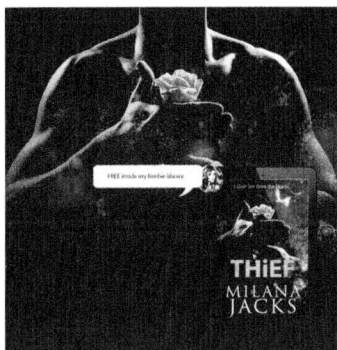

Dirty Wolf and Jake are exclusive to my newsletter subscribers
HERE!

Read the Complete Horde Series:

#1 Alpha Breeds, #2 Alpha Bonds, #3 Alpha Knots, #4 Alpha Collects

The Complete Hordesmen Series:

Hunger #1, Terror #2, Sidone #3, Fever #4, Dreikx #5, The Blind
Hordesman #6

Read the complete Beast Mates Series:

#0 Virgin - FREEBIE, #1 Blind, #2 Wild,

#2.5 Goddess, FREE via my Mailing List,

#3 Sent, #3.5 Their, #4 Caught, #4.5 His, #5 Free.

Read the complete Dragon Brotherhood:

Rise #1, Burn #2, Storm #3, Fight, #4

Short stories in IADB World: Jake 1.5, Eddy #2.5

Read the complete Age of Angels series:

Court of Command, #1 • Court of Sunder, #2 • Court of Virtue, #3

ABOUT THE AUTHOR

Milana Jacks grew up with tales of water fairies that seduced men, vampires that seduced women, and Babaroga who'd come to take her away if she didn't eat her bean soup. She writes sci-fi fantasy romance with dominant monsters from her home on Earth she shares with Mate and their three little beasts.

• Sometimes she releases stories for the readers on her mailing list as they await for books in the series. If you want in, join other readers at http://www. milanajacks.com/newsletter/ •

Meet me at
www.milanajacks.com

Printed in Great Britain
by Amazon

15861295R00088